THE
FLOOD

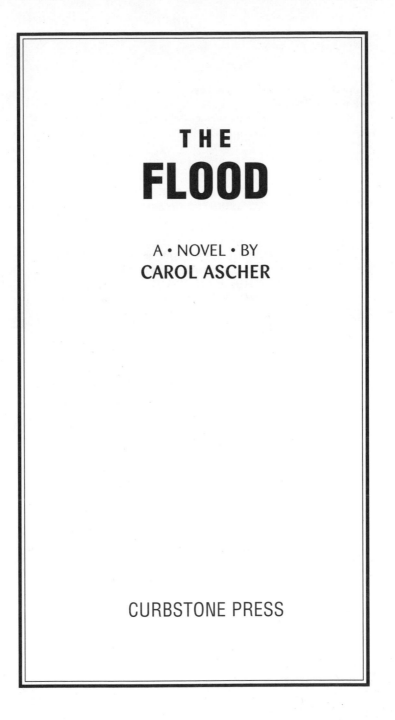

THE
FLOOD

A • NOVEL • BY
CAROL ASCHER

CURBSTONE PRESS

Printed in Canada on acid-free paper by Best Book Manufacturers
Cover by Stephanie Church

Curbstone Press is a 501(c)(3) nonprofit publishing house whose
programs are supported in part by private donations and by
grants from: ADCO Foundation, Witter Bynner Foundation for
Poetry, Connecticut Commission on the Arts, Connecticut Arts
Endowment Fund, The Ford Foundation, The Greater Hartford
Arts Council, Junior League of Hartford, Lawson Valentine
Foundation, LEF Foundation, Lila Wallace-Reader's Digest
Literary Publishers Marketing Development Program
administered by CLMP, The Andrew W. Mellon Foundation,
National Endowment for the Arts, Puffin Foundation, and United
Way-Windham Region.

Library of Congress Cataloging-in-Publication Data

Ascher, Carol, 1941-.
    The flood : a novel / by Carol Ascher.
        p.   cm.
    ISBN 1-880684-43-8
    1. Children of Holocaust survivors—Kansas—Fiction.
    2. Antisemitism—Kansas—Fiction. 3. Jews—Kansas—Fiction.
    I. Title.
    PS3551.S32F5   1996
    813'.54—dc20   96-27245

published by
CURBSTONE PRESS   321 Jackson Street   Willimantic, CT 06226
phone: (860) 423-5110   e-mail: curbston@connix.com
WWW at http://www.connix.com/~curbston/

For my Father, Paul Bergman
1907-1965

Surround yourself with rising waters:
the flood will teach you how to swim.

—Theodore Roethke

I
THE RISING WATERS

$\mathcal{I}$t was the black starry June night we had been waiting for. Each evening since spring began we had looked out at the sky as dusk fell, but either rain clouds had hung low and disturbing, or Mother had judged the ground too damp. But now, after a short drive out of Topeka in search of an empty pasture, the sky spanned high above us, filled to overflowing with stars.

"How far away is it?" I whispered. I was, as I used to say that summer, nine going on ten, and I often liked best those questions which I suspected had a very difficult answer.

"Which one, dearie?"

Father's voice was distant, as if he had moved off to join one of the stars. I didn't clarify myself. I wasn't in the mood tonight for one of Father's long explanations, part philosophy, part fact or science. Watching the black sky vibrating with stars high above me, what I might have wanted were words to release the longing the night breeze had blown over my breast.

We lay on a woolen blanket, the four of us: me, Father, Mother, and Sarah, who in fall would be seven. Sarah lay beyond Mother, on the other side of Father, but I could imagine her body curled in the crook of Mother's arm. Mother would be lying on her back, a forearm thrown across the thick wavy hair she combed back from her strong cheeks and tensely lined forehead into a roll at the nape of her neck. Perhaps she and Father, enjoying the few minutes of peace, were holding hands. Here and there lightning bugs seemed to deliver us momentary stars within our grasp, and the sound of crickets filled the air. I had told Father I was afraid that the farmer who owned the land would come with dogs to pounce on us, but Father had assured

me we were doing no harm on a plot of land left fallow. If there
were corn or wheat growing, as in the fields we had driven past,
that would be just cause for anger.

"That was the rule in Austria. It makes sense," Mother had
explained, and nostalgia filled her voice.

"But what if it's not the rule here?"

Father had laughed, and I had slowly relaxed into the night,
feeling the protection of the cool wind and stars. Still, there was
an edge of anxiety in the air.

Through my blue rimmed glasses, which forced my lazy left
eye to work as hard as my right, I searched the sky. One day in
class Miss Woody had told us that when people passed away they
became stars. This was shortly after Grandmother had died, in
winter when snow fell outside the decorated school windows and
the day seemed to wane even as we walked home, dragging our
satchels. I had not been sure Miss Woody was serious, but now
I believed her sufficiently to watch the stars dancing above me
in the hope of finding Grandmother. If the world did make a
kind of peaceful sense, as in Miss Woody's stories, Grandmother
would have been given a star next to Grandfather Hoffman, an
upright mustached man I had seen only in curling brown
photographs. He had died mysteriously in Vienna, just before
Grandmother followed my father, her son, and my mother out of
Austria to America. A nervous, aching old woman, Grandmother
had irritated my mother with her complaints each day she lived
with us. And now, some months after she had been taken in an
ambulance to the hospital where she lay in a coma and quickly
died, I had been given her lacy pink wallpapered bedroom, my
first room of my own. If I could see Grandmother among the
stars, I would know she was finally safe, and that she didn't
mind my moving in and taking over her room.

Father was explaining to Mother a suit that a Negro man was
bringing against the Board of Education; and my parents' voices,
as they talked German, blended discomfortingly with the wind.
When Grandmother was alive, Mother had reprimanded her:
"Speak English. We're in America now. In front of the children,
you must speak English." And I had felt embarrassed when,
walking down the street with them, they would forgetfully break
into German, making us stand out as sharply as when I carried

my sandwich to school on pumpernickel bread. And now, though no people were around to hear, I felt strangely disturbed by the gentle wafting of the language as Mother and Father spoke to each other. Although I could follow their conversation if I paid attention, Mother's anxiety as she softly questioned Father about the case made me want to close my ears to the German, leaving it as their private language. In daylight, Mother still said, "Psha, German, Hitler's language," and pretended she no longer wished to speak her childhood tongue. Which was also why I felt both misgiving and comfort when in the evening she and Father wrapped their thoughts in it together.

"Mummy, I can see the Big Dipper," Sarah was saying.

"*Wo, süsse?*" Mother asked.

"There!" Sarah's chubby arm pointed like a small gray branch at the sprinkled sky.

I could see the bright stars that marked out the corners of the huge ladle, to the left of the Milky Way. At home I had a little blue book on the constellations which Father and I had studied together, and most of the time I could even find Orion the Hunter and the Great Bear. The flat Kansas earth lay like a gleaming black disc beneath us, except on one side where a row of willows stood in silhouette against the horizon. There must have been a little stream nearby, for the trees always marked where water flowed.

"Daddy?" I wondered. "Did you see those same stars in Vienna?"

I looked over at Father's craggy profile outlined against the vast night. Like me and Mother, he too wore glasses. (Sarah was the only Hoffman who faced the world directly, through her fringed hazel eyes.) In the darkness, the wiry rims of Father's glasses looked like delicate pen lines which disappeared behind his large musical ears and thick black hair. Father's hair, so long compared to the men in our neighborhood, was brushed from his face, but it often flung itself stubbornly over his glasses. Then, like a shaggy dog removing a bothersome fly, he would jerk back his head. I could see Father's long fleshy nose, his sagging cheeks, and the dimple of his chin. Thinking over my question, his soft mouth seemed to stir between sorrow and humor.

"The same stars, I think, though shifted in the sky."

A dog or a wolf howled in the distance, and my body tensed against the scratchy blanket as once again I imagined the unknown farmer coming to get us. He would appear large and silhouetted at the horizon, wild dogs at his heels. Or he would suddenly stand high above us, his hands tucked in the long legs of his overalls.

Father had begun to hum a melody he sometimes played on the piano. Without the bass notes, it sounded particularly melancholy.

"Can you harmonize, dearie?" he asked.

"I don't know." A senseless worry made me fear being heard in the midst of the empty pasture. Still, I knew from my violin how to create a harmonic third. I began to hum softly along with Father.

"That's nice," Mother said from her side of the blanket.

I held my attention to the notes Father was humming and we let our voices drift with the night.

"*D*id you make your bed?" Mother asked on Thursday morning. She was standing at the living room window through which for the past minutes she had watched the glistening street.

"Yes."

I glanced up from the five-hundred piece jigsaw puzzle I was trying to turn into a picture on the coffee table. I had two sides of the frame, and part of a third. The border pieces, I had discovered, were the easiest to set in place. The box promised a red barn obscured by the profusion of an orange fall scene, when all the pieces were in.

"Because Mrs. Johnson can't clean if you haven't."

"I did, Ma." I had even hung up my pajamas and put away yesterday's clothes. I knew she was anxious to have everything in order the days Mrs. Johnson came.

Mother gave a search the length of Lindenwood toward Sixth and turned from the window. In Mrs. Johnson's honor, she had put on her nice brown and white sundress that held in her full breasts and gave a thickness to her shoulders. Wisps of dark hair had fallen out of her combs and curled damply at her neck. "The buses may be a little slow because of the heavy rain," she decided. Behind her glasses, her restless dove-gray eyes darted about the living room.

I knew nothing in the house would hold her attention until Mrs. Johnson came. I fit two leafy pieces together but they didn't connect with anything else.

"Do you intend to leave that here all day?"

"Why not?"

"It's directly in the way. How is Mrs. Johnson supposed to polish the coffee table?"

"I'll do it myself, tomorrow," I said, trying to force a piece.

"I just don't think it's very friendly—"

I scanned the border area, then the stray pieces. Sarah had come downstairs in her pajamas with the little blue bears and knelt beside me at the coffee table.

"You should get dressed," Mother told Sarah. "Mrs. Johnson is coming today."

"Just let me help Eva for a while."

"Maybe we could transfer the puzzle to a tray," Mother fretted.

"I'll ask Mrs. Johnson if she minds, when she comes," I said. It was hard to concentrate with Sarah threatening to tamper with the pieces and Mother fidgeting all over the room. She was back at the window again, her attention sucked into the empty street. I picked up a blue rabbit shape and without thinking stuck it into sky.

"That's good!" Sarah laughed.

"Maybe she forgot today is our day," Mother was muttering.

"She comes here every Thursday." Without looking up, I could feel her shaking her head, wondering whether to be hurt or angry. "She's usually a little late," I reminded Mother.

"Is she?"

"Don't move anything that's already in place," I warned Sarah, who was tinkering along the edge.

Mother came to the table and looked down, as if to join us, but then she impatiently turned away. "I should get some work done. I can't let Mrs. Johnson hold up my whole day!" she exclaimed to herself.

I moved all the red barn pieces to one side but they looked as though none would ever fit together.

I could hear Mother irritably stacking Father's books on the end table next to the couch, and then she went across the room to the piano and neatened our music scores. She thought Father and I should store our compositions inside the piano bench when we were finished, but we hardly ever put them away. She had stuffed my violin in the corner and was starting to fold my music rack, which was really silly, and she wasn't quite sure how and got it stuck half way. Finally, she tucked it in the corner. Then she turned and faced us, arms folded awkwardly, from the other side of the room.

"It's unfair that poor people have to work hard for others, and sometimes, *natürlich*, they resent it," she announced. "I try to pay Mrs. Johnson well. Still, it's not a good wage. So, that's the reason that occurs to me she might be taking her time."

"She's not that late," I said.

"Yes, but you did mention that she always comes a little late." A shadow of distress crossed Mother's worried face. "And here, in America, the poor are almost always Negroes."

"We don't have to have a cleaning lady," I said, wishing that we wouldn't bring this added sorrow and confusion into our house. Today Mother was worse than usual, but she was always agitated the mornings Mrs. Johnson came. "I don't see why we even have one."

"We always had somebody at home in Vienna—more than one. Country women who even lived with us. *Ach*! I don't know. It's hard with two children!"

"Mrs. Johnson has four children," I said.

"Mother gave me a hurt look and went to stick her head out the front door. "Ah hah! Here she comes," she cried, and her voice was suddenly pitched high with the pleasure of her strange victory. "But she doesn't even have an umbrella! I should go out and bring her one!" She came back inside, almost giggly with relief, grabbed an umbrella, and disappeared out the door.

"Mama's cuckoo around Mrs. Johnson," Sarah noted.

I didn't say anything. It was hard not to snap at Mother when she was so out of kilter. But the worst thing was, with everyone being tense, sometimes I couldn't even figure out if I liked Mrs. Johnson.

"Here she is, here she is!" Mother called out gaily. She held the door open for Mrs. Johnson and shook out the umbrella.

Mrs. Johnson was wearing a dark raincoat, and her black hair was wound around her head in a tight braided crown. She had fine small almost Oriental eyes and a soft upper lip that was tulip-like, pretty, when she wasn't tired or annoyed. She was carrying her work clothes in a large plastic bag. When, some years earlier, she had first come to our house, she had also brought along her lunch in a paper bag each time, but Mother had slowly convinced her to eat whatever we were eating along with us.

"Hi," I said, hobbling up from my puzzle, caught by a leg that had quietly fallen asleep.

"Morning, Eva, Sarah," Mrs. Johnson nodded. She took off her coat and handed it to Mother.

I was prancing on my numb leg, and then it began to bristle inside. "Want to see our puzzle?" I bounded to and fro.

Mrs. Johnson came over to the table. Her bright orange traveling dress was decorated with a rhinestone pin at the neck. The sheath hung loosely over her thin body, and you could see her collar bone and the tiny horizontal ribs above her breast. She concentrated on the puzzle momentarily, bent over, and, with her long dark, large knuckled fingers, snapped a piece of tree into place.

Laughing, I dropped to my knees to begin work again.

"Would you like a cup of coffee?" Mother asked, coming toward us.

"No thanks. "I s'pose I'm late enough as it is."

"I was worried about you!"

Mrs. Johnson's black eyes snapped at Mother under half-closed lids. "It wastes my time too when the bus driver don't stop."

"What?"

"That driver, he just went right by."

"You could skip some of the ironing," Mother shook her head worriedly. "That way you can still go home on time."

"That ain't the point. I can stay to finish your ironing. It's just that they done that to me before. Them drivers don't think a nickel from colored folks is worth the same as a nickel from you whites."

"Maybe he didn't see you," Mother suggested hesitantly.

"Oh, he saw me. He saw me all right! I run after him waving and yelling as he drove away. Then I had to come all the way back to the stop and wait twenty more minutes in the rain." She looked down at the puzzle, as if ready to move another piece into place, and then seemed to pull herself back, remembering that she was at our house to clean. "Well, I'd best be getting to work."

"*Ach*! I don't understand this country," Mother shuddered.

"It ain't a country fixed for colored folks, that's for sure."

"Why can't people understand we're *alle Menschen*, all human beings." Mother's eyes were red at the rims.

"Tch! You Jewish people be thinking that way," Mrs. Johnson said to Mother, and picked up her shopping bag.

Mother rubbed her finger behind her glasses. "Would you like me to report the driver to the bus company?"

Mrs. Johnson lowered her eyes; she often got standoffish when Mother wanted to go out of her way to help.

"I hope you don't think that's interfering," Mother said cautiously. "But people shouldn't get away with injustice like that."

"I don't suppose it would hurt," Mrs. Johnson agreed, turning to go upstairs to change. "They're not likely to listen to me. Course if a white lady complains she can't get her help on time—"

Mrs. Johnson's piece of tree had opened up new possibilities, and I worked steadily on the puzzle. I could hear Mother talking to the bus company on the telephone. Her voice was curt and choppy with the anxiety of talking to authorities in English. When she was through she began to move about here and there, calm at last to have Mrs. Johnson safely in our house. Sarah went to take off her pajamas for the day, and I followed her upstairs.

Mrs. Johnson was in the bathroom, scrubbing out the sink. She had changed into her fluffy slippers and an old print cleaning dress that had once been Mother's. A yellow bandanna covered her ebony crown of braids and made her dark face look pinched and worn. Mrs. Johnson, I decided, not for the first time, was altogether different from the warm black mammies of my children's books. First, she was much too thin; next, she tended to be irritable and did not hesitate to complain. Actually, she reminded me of my grandmother, who had often knocked us off her lap with impatience when we tried to scramble on. Both had aches in their arms and legs, which was why, I supposed, they were so often tired and cross.

"You got a safety pin for me?" she asked, eyeing me at the door. "I already broke a button on this old rag."

I looked down at the dress, trying to imagine the way Mother's stocky form had once filled it out. "I think so."

My bedroom had been wonderfully papered according to Grandmother's taste in pink with vertical stripes of white lace, threaded with light blue ribbons. When Grandmother was alive, I would sometimes sit on the edge of her bed and challenge her to guess the number of blue bows from floor to ceiling or across from wall to wall. Now I stopped to peer into the depth of the lace, and found myself floating into a dreamy pink world, soft and endless, but held in by the snowflake doorways. Pulling myself away and back toward duty, I sprinkled colored food shavings into the glass bowl for the goldfish, who came swimming up to the surface, their mouths moving like Grandmother's when she took out her teeth at night. On the bookcase next to the bowl was a little candy box I had stuffed with velvet in the hope of creating a jewelry box: a few pennies, a paper clip, and a piece of yo-yo string were hidden among the folds of cloth, but no safety pin. I fingered a little gold violin brooch someone had given me. Mrs. Johnson could pin her dress with that. *The Secret Garden* lay face down on my bed, drawing me to its mysterious old mansion on the moor. But I went back into the bathroom and handed her the brooch.

"Thanks," she said, and put down her wet rag. "The button was so old it broke off too small to be any good." She held her bodice together and pushed the pin through. She seemed to be complaining about Mother's hand-me-down.

"You can have it," I said.

"Oh, I don't want to take no pin of yours. I'll give it back at the end of the day."

"Really, you can have it," I said, settling on the rim of the bathtub. "I don't like violin pins that much."

Mrs. Johnson looked down at her bodice to examine the pin as decoration, and I couldn't tell if she would accept the brooch. Then she ran hot water over her rag and began wiping the mirror over the sink with vigorous, angry strokes.

"You girls spit at the mirror?" she stopped to rub at a tooth-paste splotch.

"I don't think so," I giggled nervously.

"Seems you girls can't be getting that much toothpaste in your mouth, all that ends up on the mirror."

I tried to imagine brushing my teeth with my mouth closed so that nothing spattered. Still, there was something comforting in having Mrs. Johnson find fault.

"What are your children doing for summer vacation?" I asked.

"The three boys is doing one thing and my girl is doing something else."

"What is Mayella doing?" I had never seen the girl, whom I imagined as slim and lovely with her mother's dark sloping eyes.

Mrs. Johnson was wiping the glass ledge above the sink where we kept our toothpaste and water glasses. As she looked over, her suspicion seemed to relax and her eyes softened into something close to affection. "Mayella be babysitting most days."

"Mayella," I repeated, liking the name. "Does Mayella like to read?"

"She's a cracker jack reader!" Mrs. Johnson nodded to herself. "I can't hardly get her away from a book when I'm at home. She's going to be a school teacher when she grows up, for sure."

"Does she ever read *The Secret Garden*?"

"I don't know. I'll tell you, though, that girl can read like a preacher. She reads to the children where she babysits. She's gonna teach school like her aunt—my husband's sister." Mrs. Johnson gave me her determined look.

"Where will she teach?" I asked, suddenly realizing that there were no Negro teachers in our school. In fact, though I'd never quite noticed, there were no Negro children.

"She'll teach in one of our colored schools," Mrs. Johnson said. "Same as Lureen—unless Reverend Brown changes all that." A strange expression, part fear part hope, worked the muscles of her narrow face. Then she turned away from me to scrub the faucets.

"What do you mean?" I persisted.

"Well, Lureen already got her notice from the Board of Education. I'm not speaking against the Reverend, don't get me wrong! But the Board wrote her contract is terminated on account of they may not need her services in the colored schools if Reverend Brown wins his suit.

Mrs. Johnson's complicated explanation made my head buzz. "What about the boys?" I asked, returning to a simpler subject.

"Lebert, Edmund and John Henry," she recited, methodically rubbing.

"What do they do while you're gone all day?"

"Oh, mostly they all go about on their own. Lebert and Edmund, they work some days on the farm near us." She twisted the water out of her rag. "They're supposed to be out harvesting wheat today, except that the rain has delayed everything so bad. So I don't know what they're doing, the three of them—wasting time, I s'pect. I don't even know if there'll be wheat to harvest if the rain keeps up."

"Why not?"

"Hessian flies and root rot," she said, coming over to the tub and turning the spigot on full force. I slid down to the far end, away from the thick stream. Mrs. Johnson was on her hands and knees in front of the tub and, as her slippers fell away, the pink soles of her feet stood out like the delicate peonies in our side yard. They were the same pink color I'd seen deep inside her mouth the few times she'd let herself loose in happy abandoned laughter. She began to attack the gray line that formed each week half way up the bathtub rim.

"How come it's raining so much?" I asked. "Why do you think?"

She gave me an impatient look. "The rainmakers, I s'pect."

"Who's that?"

"The rainmakers. Them white folks that gets up in airplanes to move the clouds along. The farmer my boys work for saw them in their planes earlier this spring.

"Where were the clouds before?"

Mrs. Johnson had spattered the bathtub with cleanser. As she scrubbed the deep basin with her soapy rag, her long brown hands turned gray and her large knuckles looked swollen and creased.

"Maybe you could bring Mayella with you sometime," I said.

"Maybe."

"I could show her my books."

"Uh huh."

I studied her thin chest, swaying with each stroke; she was as small as a girl through the middle—as narrow as book-loving Mayella would be; and Mother's loose dress, held together with pins, made her so frail.

"That brooch looks nice on you," I said, wanting to protect her with something of mine.

She touched the pin on her dress, and for a moment her lips flowered and were lovely and full. Then her mouth hardened into a fine line and she flapped the rag. "Your mama's gonna miss it and ask you where it went."

I imagined telling Mother I had given the violin to Mrs. Johnson. "She won't mind," I lied.

"Move off there, I got to do the tub where you're sitting."

But actually, if I didn't tell Mother, she wouldn't even notice it was gone. "I hardly ever wear the pin. You can have it, really."

"Eva, you be quiet, or I'm going to take it off right now," said Mrs. Johnson, giving me a cutting glance and beginning to scrub the final section of the tub where I had been sitting."

*O*ne drizzly day, when by late afternoon Sarah and I had exhausted ourselves across the street in front of Mrs. Rogers' new TV, Mother bundled us into our yellow raincoats and sent us off on the bus to pick up Father at the private psychiatric sanitarium where he worked most days. As we climbed down at the Menninger's stop, a light rain was misting the air, glazing each blade of grass. Several nurses walked arm in arm with their patients along the paths. While we pulled off our raincoats and tucked them under our arms, I surveyed the tightly cut lawn in the direction of Father's pink building. In those days, I was always on the lookout for patients Father had pointed out to me: one was able to live with his family in town, because he had been helped to stop making an obscene gesture and now touched his thumb with one finger after the other in endless succession.

"There's Lillian," I whispered to Sarah, and felt my breath contract. I nodded toward the colorful figure on a nearby bench, bent like a red and green snow man over her scribbling pad.

"Euuu!" Sarah held her yellow slicker tightly and clutched my arm.

The sight of Lillian made my hands clammy. Yet she was my favorite of the crazy ones, and I didn't want to miss her.

"You think she'll hurt us?" Sarah opened wide her eyes.

"Don't be silly." This was Father's voice inside me: mentally ill people aren't really dangerous, he liked to say; it's both unfortunate and lucky that the people their misery makes them hurt most are themselves.

We were next to her, and Lillian had reached out as usual to grasp my hand. She had short fingers with fiery red nails, but the polish had worn off and was jagged at the dirty tips. Her hand, as moist as my own, seemed to meet indistinguishably with mine.

Suspicious green eyes darted out from a face as puffy as a white dinner roll, while she said something under her breath I couldn't understand.

"What?"

"Don't let them tell you it's not the rain." Her voice was barely audible.

"I think it's stopping now," I answered shakily. I liked the adventure of testing my steady mind, that and getting close to unexpected thoughts, so out of the ordinary, so strange.

"Forty days and forty nights," exclaimed Lillian, suddenly loud enough for anyone quite far away to hear, and then she lowered to a near whisper: "The Lord repented that he made man, and it grieved him at his heart."

"Huh?" I didn't know what she was talking about.

"The rain will take us all!" Lillian laughed. Her red hair lay in matted snaky curls all over her head. "It grieved him. It grieved him! It's going to rain and rain, you know," she confided. She giggled girlishly, showing the queer space between her front teeth.

A pool of moisture was forming in the clasp of our hands. I wanted to release my fingers but was afraid to hurt Lillian by withdrawing from her grasp. Even though Lillian was crazy, she was still an adult, and I was only a child. I could feel Sarah on my other side, tugging at my raincoat.

"It's supposed to be sunny part of tomorrow," I said.

"If it's sunny, it'll be rainy sun. The sun will melt and turn to rain. Golden rain falling down!" An eerie giggle issued from somewhere inside her, as she gazed directly into my eyes. "It grieves him. Wickedness is so great upon the earth! No one can stop it now!"

"A sun can't turn to rain," Sarah said disdainfully, but she was clutching my raincoat.

"Too much filth. Everywhere wickedness, filth and lies!"

I shuddered slightly.

Then, as if Lillian had pulled an altogether different personality from the mist, she dropped my fingers and sighed peacefully. "Sisters. What's your name, dear?"

"Eva. Eva Hoffman." I wiped my hand on my pinafore. "I've told you before. And she's Sarah."

"Yes." Lillian looked down at her writing pad, then glanced up. "How's your mother, dear?"

My mind leaped to the shadow of Mother as she had stood behind the screen door, saying goodbye to us. "Fine," I said cautiously.

"What's a woman to do when every hole comes unplugged!" Lillian bent over to write on her pad.

At the far end of the walk, the mauve door to the building opened, and Father and his friend, Mordecai, appeared in their seersucker suits. They were talking intently and then tall lean Helene, who was a social worker, came out the door and started talking excitedly to the two. She was the tallest woman I knew, and stood high above the men. Looking across the lawn, she saw me and waved; then she went back inside.

"That's my dad," I said proudly.

Lillian scratched her ear with a chipped fingernail and squinted at the entrance as if she were extremely nearsighted.

"I know the man," she confided, and lapsed into a confused mix of words I couldn't understand.

"Daddy's not afraid of the rain," Sarah said, and skipped off to join Father.

I stood next to Lillian, suddenly calm and peaceful as Father and Mordecai came towards us. Father and Mordecai were the two men I loved most in the world. Best friends, they had been together all my life. When they walked side by side, everything came to its light center around them. Mordecai's hair seemed even blacker than Father's, partly because he had a thick black beard. While Father's sturdy frame gave the impression of a tree trunk that pulls downward toward the ground in search of water for its roots, Mordecai was light and slim: his shoulders were narrow and a little hunched inside his suit; a fall he had taken as a child in Prague made him lurch skyward as he walked. When I wasn't angry at Father, I admired him enormously—he seemed to know and understand so much; Mordecai was also smart and wise, but beyond this, something made him mysterious: Mordecai was a quietly religious man.

Sarah had joined them and was now skipping toward me and Lillian, tucked snugly between Mordecai and Father.

"What are you writing?" I buried my excitement at their approach and looked down at Lillian's pad. Tiny words had been rapidly scribbled in all directions.

"Notes for the confessor," she answered, and fearfully covered her hand over her pad. "A record." She looked up at me and cackled at some tricky joke.

"Hello Lillian," Father greeted her. He rested his solid hand on my shoulder.

If Mordecai hadn't been there, I would have nuzzled my head against Father's chest. As it was, I gave a shy upward smile that encompassed them both.

"Father Hoffman, is that man Father Stone?" Lillian was shuffling the soiled scraps of paper of her writing pad.

"Yah, Mort Stone," Mordecai said, his Czech accent forming his last name as if it were Schtone. He reached out his hand to Lillian, "But I'm not a priest."

Lillian leaned forward to shake hands but then shifted as if she would grab Father's jacket. Suddenly she seemed agitated again. Her green eyes were flashing and her fingers moved as rapidly as birds. "I tell the priest about the rain, but he doesn't listen. I tell him it grieves the Lord—forty days and forty nights! You think he listens? He doesn't understand the mess we're in. And with all his fine education!" she crowed. "Violence and corruption. What does he think? It can go on forever? I don't care. Why should I be afraid after what I've been through? He once meant to come on earth in heavenly glory, but we sinned! So he came in weakness, not in power. You think that did any good? I don't even expect to be among the survivors. But I'm beginning to think I need a lawyer rather than a priest." She caught the flight of her hand in mid air and bit a dirty nail. Then she looked up at them, searching their faces.

"Lawyers have never been very good at either morality or the weather," Father smiled.

"You know that after the flood God promised he would never again destroy the world by water," Mordecai added, nodding thoughtfully.

Lillian looked skeptical, near anger.

"Remember? He made a. . . how do you call it, a covenant with his bow," Mordecai explained. "He made a rainbow appear in a cloud. That was his promise that he would never again destroy everything by flood."

"He didn't know at the time how bad it would get," Lillian insisted, and inside her puffy face her eyes glowered.

Father laughed.

"Really!" It seemed for an instant that Lillian would stand up and grab Father by the collar. But then, crossing herself, she said, "Oh my God! I am so heartily sorry," and let out an awful cackle.

I moved away cautiously, shifting my raincoat.

"We have to go home now, Lillian," Father touched her shoulder. "Water is always frightening. But the rain will have a limit."

We walked on, back along the path that crossed the lawn to the street and the bus stop. I nestled in with Sarah between Father and Mordecai and took Father's hand.

"The benefits of religion." Father raised his eyebrows at Mordecai.

"What was the name of Noah's wife?" Lillian called after us.

"Hm. I don't remember," said Mordecai. Ignoring Father's sarcasm, he turned back and lifted his arms in puzzlement.

"You two doctors Jewish?" she called again.

"Now what does she want?" Mordecai asked Father, and put his forefinger to his mouth to warn Lillian not to yell on hospital grounds.

"Maybe she thinks that Jews have some inside knowledge," Father mused. "I'd forgotten there was never supposed to be another flood."

"A fire when the world ends. I didn't want to remind her of Hiroshima and Nagasaki. They seem more apropos, if one is predicting the Armageddon." Mordecai brushed the black hairs of his beard away from his soft pink mouth. "Or maybe the camps with their smell of flesh rising with the smoke."

"Oh, come," Father said impatiently. "Do you have to make the Jews the vanguard of everything?"

"You don't think there are some advantages of being the 'chosen people'?" Mordecai grinned.

"Hitler took his inspiration from what the Turks did to the Armenians—a fine massacre about which no one cared!"

"I don't see very many people caring about the Jews. Anyway, if we're talking about the end of the world, there's the atom bomb," Mordecai nodded, more to himself than to Father. "Apparently they now say we can't win in Korea without bombing the Chinese." He was pulling his beard with slow methodical strokes." "The lady has obviously studied the Bible, but it would be hard to disentangle what comes from where."

Father shrugged with annoyance. "Why Hans has the patience for her, I don't understand. He must have learned endurance sitting in that chicken coop, waiting for the War to end. To me, it doesn't make sense, letting her talk that mixture of Catholic school and the weather page year after year."

"Helene was actually talking to me earlier today about transferring several patients to the State Hospital."

"Good. If Lillian's family weren't so filthy rich, none of us would have agreed to Hans wasting five precious hours each week listening to her rubbish for this long."

Father sounded righteous and mean. I glanced up: his jowls were heavy and loose, and his eyes were far away behind his glasses."

"Helene was upset at some of the transfers. I don't agree with most of them either. Luckily Hans doesn't think Lillian's a waste of time," said Mordecai.

The distance between him and Father seemed to waver and widen as they walked.

"Sometimes this clinic seems like a high class resort with special esoteric services," Father laughed bitterly. "*Der Zauberberg* in the middle of the prairie. Americans, of course, will try any route to salvation—religion, psychoanalysis, soap."

"The world is very dirty!" Sarah called out, flashing her eyes and snapping her fingers awkwardly in imitation of Lillian.

"Yah, I'm very glad Hans doesn't mind treating her," Mordecai smiled at Sarah.

"I couldn't stand it," Father shook his head.

"Very dirty!" Sarah repeated, grinning up at us, Lillian-like.

"That's enough, Sarah," said Father, trying not to show he was amused.

"Why Daddy?" I asked. "Why wouldn't you want to take care of her?"

"Your father doesn't think there is hope for her to get well," explained Mordecai. "He's turning into a cynic."

Father flinched and seemed to retreat into himself, but then he looked sharply at Mordecai. "I don't know what interesting breakthrough you're waiting for. The woman hasn't made progress since she arrived here five, maybe six, years ago. There is no way to break into her obsessions—Hans will admit it! She's even a little worse now than when she came. Last winter she had that cockeyed theory about a glacial flow coming down from Canada; now it's the flood. Always the weather to punish us or cover over our sins. I suppose you're pleased that the Old Testament God is as strong in her as the New." Father's face relaxed into whimsy and he chuckled despite himself.

"It grieves the Lord," Sarah shot out, waving her arms. Once she started imitating, you couldn't stop her.

"Good Sarah, you make a nice crazy woman," Father smiled.

"It's lucky her family has money. If all life grants her is such slow deterioration, at least it's more pleasant here than over at the State Hospital," Mordecai decided. "You didn't take your car today?"

"But I'm not crazy, am I?" demanded Sarah.

"No," said Father, to Mordecai and Sarah.

"Lillian isn't going to die?" I asked worriedly.

"No, we didn't mean that. She's very healthy, physically," Father assured me.

"But she isn't really unhappy, is she?" I asked. With her swift mood swings, Lillian seemed to fly with great speed high over the emotions I knew.

"Deep down she's probably living in quite a hell," Mordecai said.

That idea wasn't the least comforting. "Was she peculiar before she went crazy?" I now wanted to know.

"A little, maybe. She had three children, and after each birth she seemed to find it harder to pull herself back together."

"She isn't very old, is she?"

"About your mother's age, maybe," said Mordecai.

The idea was frightening. I had thought of Lillian as old. "But Mother hasn't gotten sick from having Sarah and me," I insisted, more to Father.

"No, not at all," he laughed.

"So once again we argue over what people have a right to expect from the world," Mordecai was saying to Father.

Shaking his head, Father took my hand; his palm was warm and dry. "I was just thinking that," he said.

The rain was beginning to come down again, wetting our arms and shoulders. We put on our yellow slickers and hurried to the bus shelter by the road. Sarah, who seemed to have forgotten about Lillian, picked up pebbles and threw them at the puddles the rain was forming in the gravel at the edge of the street. I wanted to ask what had happened to Lillian's children, but I could tell I had reached my limit and Father would be impatient with more questions. Mordecai had taken out his pipe and was filling it with the little leaves of sweet-smelling tobacco while he and Father talked.

*T*here were days that summer when the sky hung over us like a monstrous dark water balloon someone had pricked. Father was showing me stories in the newspaper about the flooding of little towns. First a tributary of the Kansas River began to swell and overflow Salina—that was still over one hundred miles away. A few days later, Abilene flooded, and then the Kaw itself began to fill to overflowing, and places like Manhattan were covered over by a few feet of muddied water. The aerial photographs in the paper showed a vast, boundless lake extending peacefully in all directions, with only a row of trees or several roof tops to indicate the life below. I had in my mind Lillian's prediction, but was afraid to say it. Then one day as Father sat over the newspaper, I asked.

"Do you think Lillian's right that everything will be covered over by a flood?"

"No, crazy people don't predict events," Father laughed ruefully into his paper. "Their minds just take in whatever is going on and they jumble it up with other things they want or are afraid of."

"But the water is getting higher everywhere."

"True."

I had set a little tin pan outside my window, at Father's suggestion. With it, I measured the inches of water that fell each night. In the morning, I moved sleepily to the foot of my bed and knelt at the window to watch the rain that poured down in silvery slats onto the roof and formed tiny whirling eddies in my little tin pan. Sometimes a Baltimore oriole or a robin stood out in the garden below, taking advantage of a pool in the soggy lawn to enjoy a private bath. Windshield wipers slapped back and forth as a car made its way along the back street, and the sky had a heavy quality that was neither night nor day.

"How much water do you think we got this week?" Sarah asked. She liked the idea of gauging things exactly, and had taken to coming in her pajamas straight from her bed onto mine.

"Two and a half inches!" Sarah peered out the window at the measuring rod stuck in the pan. "I bet we won't be able to go out and play again today," she complained, and stuck her thumb in her mouth.

I pulled her dimpled hand away from her face. She had finally stopped sucking her thumb last summer after Mother put Louisiana hot sauce on it, and was only doing it again because of the rain. "Don't do that."

"Will we?" she insisted, peering out at me from under her drooping bangs.

I closed my eyes and listened to the sounds of rain hitting the roof under my window. The rain made me melancholy, even when I didn't have important thoughts on my mind. I was reading *The Raft,* a book whose jacket picture of five men crowded on a tiny raft in a stormy ocean had caught my eye in the public library. Sometimes I didn't even read the book but just lay on my bed and stared at the cover. I had never seen an ocean, and tried to imagine the thick salt water the men in the book were afraid to drink. They waited for rain, and when it came, opened their mouths to the sky like birds; after weeks without food, they worried that they might starve and talked about eating each other if one of them died.

"Would you ever eat anyone?" I asked Sarah.

"What?" She looked at me quizzically.

"Would you ever eat anyone?"

"You mean, a live person?"

"Or a dead one."

Sarah took a playful bite out of the air. Then she shrugged nonchalantly, "I don't know."

I was longing for a sister with whom I could share my moody thoughts on cannibalism and other difficult topics. When I talked about ideas with Father, his views twisted mine in his direction before they were strong enough to live on their own. But Sarah baffled me. It wasn't just that she was younger. She had an entirely different kind of brain: instead of snuggling into stormy thoughts as I did, she brushed them off and walked away. Sometimes she seemed like a complete stranger, even though she was a sister who crept into my bed every morning. "You should take my question seriously," I reprimanded her. "You might have to make a decision about eating a person sometime, if you were really hungry."

"I would eat a dog," she said, trying to be nice.

"Sarah!" I said, "That's not the point."

I could feel Mother in the doorway, and then she cried out, "Look who's in Eva's bed again!"

I glanced back at her. She had put on her glasses and brushed her hair, so that her face was screened and tidy, but her body was still lumpy in her faded bathrobe.

"Soon you both will ask to be back in the same room together," she laughed happily at us.

Instinctively, I pushed Sarah's hand from where it rested on the window ledge.

"Don't," Sarah squirmed, and replaced her pudgy hand.

Mother came toward the bed; as she stood looking out the window, her warm sour smell of sleep filled the air.

"Mummy, we had almost a full tin today—two and a half inches," Sarah said brightly.

"That's a lot," Mother agreed.

"Mrs. Johnson said the rain is the fault of the rainmakers," I told her, keeping to myself Lillian's more murky and disturbing explanation. I wasn't even sure what kinds of wickedness Lillian had meant.

"Who are the rainmakers?" Sarah asked.

"She said it's men who get up in planes and move the clouds from one place to another. She said they got paid to move them all over here."

"Nature should be left to nature," Mother shook her head violently, and stared out at the yard. By the garage, deep gullies had formed in the flower beds. "Nature should be left to nature," she repeated, with less certainty. "We have more than enough work to take care of people."

"What do you mean?" I asked.

"You children lead a pleasant life, but there are many things you haven't seen."

I shrugged; I didn't like the way Mother tried to make me feel bad about vague things I hadn't experienced or were too far away for me to know.

"Integration," Mother announced, suddenly finding her topic and growing sure of herself. "Now some courageous people are working to change the law so that Negro children can go to school with everyone else. I don't know if you saw the paper. A Mr. Brown, the father of a little girl almost your age, is suing the Board of Education because she has to travel on a bus all the way across town when there is a perfectly good school on her street. Even your daddy's friend Helene is going to help." Mother looked at me, but her mind was racing with her own thoughts. "How can it be that in America these Negro children should be separated from all others? You can't tell one group to go to another school, or forbid them from attending school altogether. That's what the Nazis did in Austria! All people are the same under the sun! Everyone is alike!" Her voice strained with the importance of her fragile message, as she peered out at the rain. "What is good enough for one group is good enough for another. No group of people is so special they can keep others out."

"Ma!" I said. Her wild flow of feelings made me want to push her away or dive into the cool safety of the pink lace. "Anyway, Mrs. Johnson already told me about that," I said, vaguely remembering the name Brown.

"Until the world is safe for all people, it's not safe for any group," Mother continued, not hearing. "We Jews know that. Until we are all equal, no one is—"

"Ma!" I said more sharply; I had heard this from her many times. "I already know that."

"Okay," she agreed sadly, and turned from the window. "But you should also care about these things. It's important that I don't raise stupid, uncaring children." And then, as if she suddenly heard what I had said a moment earlier, she fearfully asked, "What did Mrs. Johnson say?"

"She said," I tried quickly to remember. "I think, because of Mr. Brown, he's a minister, well Lureen—that's her sister-in-law—might not have a school to teach in."

"*Ach*!" Mother shook her head. "*Schwein*! Still, Mrs. Johnson can't be against integration."

"She didn't talk about that," I said, unsure of what the word meant.

"Everybody should be allowed to be together, black and white," Mother insisted.

I let my eyes swim over the walls, wondering whether to count the blue ribbons. "Mrs. Johnson's children don't *have* to go to a special school for Negro children, do they?" I asked, gripping the blue with terrifying certainty of what the answer would be.

"The law says they do, young lady," Mother said, and her eyes swam with righteous hurt behind her glasses.

I pictured how I had sat on the rim of the bathtub while Mrs. Johnson scrubbed, and the bottoms of her feet had been so delicate and pink. "Why didn't she say so?" I demanded, feeling betrayed.

"I'm sure she thinks you know. This is a segregated state!"

I could sense a shameful blush rising in my cheeks. What had Mrs. Johnson said about Mayella? Or John Henry and the other boys?

"Some of the kids in school say nigger," I blurted, and the blush bloomed hot in my cheeks.

"*Ach*!" Mother shook her head in pain.

For a while the three of us were quiet together as we watched the rain banging the ground like hard nails. Then I glanced up at Mother. Her determined face was strained with worry, or with holding back an unbearable worry. I had seen that look before. What came to my mind was a morning when Sarah, at two years old, had tumbled down the basement stairs. Then Sarah's mouth oozed blood, and a fear twisted Mother's face, even though she said over and over that soon Sarah would be as good as new. Even now, as Sarah's baby teeth were beginning to wiggle, Mother steeled herself whenever she looked into Sarah's mouth to make sure her permanent teeth would come in straight.

On Sunday the sky hung like a high luminous gray silk cloth overhead that gave a breathing space to the world below. The air smelled sweet, and the birds were chirping noisily in relief from the rain. Father, Sarah and I strolled the few blocks of sidewalks to the end of Lindenwood and, when the sidewalk ended, followed the curb past the older wooden houses with large farm-like gardens, neighborhoods that seemed neither city nor country. A cow here, a flock of chickens there, stared curiously at us from their muddy homes behind fences. We were the only people in town who walked, and even the animals thought us odd. We had rounded the corner of a rickety old house half hidden by vine and walked the length of a spongy rutted road when, in the distance, I could see the electric poles along the line of the Rock Island Railroad tracks. It was near here that Sarah and I had counted over one hundred cars on a steadily moving freight train, while Mother looked away, refusing to tell me why the long line of freight cars so upset her. Now the wooden cross ties lay on the soggy land like soaked planks across a marsh. We cautiously treaded our way over them, then climbed up a slight incline. From there we gazed at the river, which had widened into an endless shallow lake. Grass waved like delicate seaweed under water, and bits of garbage floated like sad ducks. At the muddy water's edge, Sarah peeled off her shoes and socks and went wading, while Father and I stood looking on.

"It's lucky no one has a house right here," I said to him, taking his hand.

"True," Father nodded, and pointed eastward along the horizon. "But over there, look, you can see, half a dozen houses are under water."

I gazed out at the houses: faraway, they appeared like tiny building blocks resting in the water. So the Kaw really was flooding, and it was pouring itself over our town!

"Are those people still in their houses?" I asked.

Father shook his head; he looked sullen and heavy-hearted. "I don't see how they could be. They've probably moved in with relatives or friends."

"Yuk," I winced.

"You know, this river floods every twenty-five years or so." He combed his fingers through his thick hair. "There was a bad flood in 1925, also one in 1907. People on both sides of the river lost practically everything. The water we see now is very little compared to what happened then. After the last big flood, there was apparently talk of building dikes, which would have prevented this, but nothing was ever done."

"Who told you this?" I asked indignantly.

"Mostly I read it in the paper." Father smiled, but his lips were turned down at the edges. "And people at the clinic who've been here a long time, as well as Mr. Cotter next door, told me the same thing."

"Why did people go back to their houses after the last time the river flooded?"

"Not everyone can afford to move," said Father.

"But it's been happening over and over," I exclaimed.

"You might as well ask why the city didn't build a dike."

"Daddy!"

"You want to know about the individual families? People's memories fade," said Father. "When the water recedes, they go back to their homes, or new people move in, and life returns to normal."

"But they're only going to lose more money if they stay where they are and everything gets destroyed again!"

Mother had called Mrs. Johnson, who had said, though water was filling the basement, her house still seemed safe. She had also told Mother how her house had been hit by the earlier flood. Why hadn't she moved elsewhere—for instance, onto the street near us where a few Negroes lived in small brightly-trimmed homes?

"That's why poor people stay poor. They live in endangered areas where they're more likely to lose everything, but they can never accumulate the savings to move."

"Mrs. Johnson's sister-in-law is a teacher," I reported, as if this might bring hope.

"That's nice." He looked confused. "Does she live by the river?"

"I don't know," I mumbled. "But she's not a cleaning lady."

"Even Negro teachers don't make as much money as white teachers," Father said sadly.

The idea was too unfair to settle in my mind; but it might have its brighter side. "Then the Board of Education should be happy to bring them into the white schools," I cried, as if, given the bargain she offered, Lureen Johnson would surely not be fired.

Father didn't answer for a moment. Then he spat out, "That contract stuff is just pure intimidation."

"You mean Lureen Johnson won't be fired after all?"

"That's her name? I don't know."

"Why doesn't she move to another city?"

"Because it's not much better for a Negro anywhere in this country."

"Or out of the country then—like you did!" I cried.

Father nodded ambiguously.

"Still, anyone can move away from the river!" I insisted, as I looked out over the waters: what if Negro teachers, who had also lost their jobs, lived in those little submerged houses?

"You're a very smart young lady. Maybe you should go and advise them." Father gave a slight ironic smile.

"No, come on, Daddy!" I wanted a solution that would not only settle the past, but make our school and the present waters alter their apparently immutable course.

"Dearie, people don't want to move like that. They have ties to their homes." Father's gray eyes tightened behind his wiry glasses.

"I'd move right away if anything happened," I assured him. "No matter how much money I had." Still, it nagged at me that for the second time Mrs. Johnson was staying quietly in her home.

"Maybe you would. But it's not so easy, even if you have enough money. Even Mother and I really waited too long before we ran from Vienna. I would see something intolerable or hear of an acquaintance who had just disappeared. But then life would quiet down and I would forget, even be hopeful; or I would grow used to what had initially been an unbearable humiliation. It took the Germans marching into Vienna to make things clear in a new way."

As usual, I was having a hard time picturing Vienna. "Like what kind of humiliation did you get used to?"

"Oh, not riding the streetcar, or using the public park. Sometimes they just hauled Jews off the street and beat them up. Things not so different than what they do to the Negroes here."

"But what happened that made you leave?" I demanded, rushing on to picture firmly that special moment that led one to choose for sure safety and dry land.

Father rubbed his stubby cheeks as if to bring them circulation. "Be careful you don't cut yourself on a can," he called to Sarah.

She stood and gave us a winning smile. "I won't. I'm making a pile—I already have eleven. You want to help?" she yelled at me.

"No," I shook my head, then turned to Father, hiding my fear: "What?"

Father nodded, collecting his thoughts, fixing his eyes on the immense brownish bubbling river as he prepared to talk. "Well, as I said, the Nazis had invaded," he began finally, still looking over the water. "So everyone was looking for new countries to immigrate to. But there was one incident that made it all different to me. I was walking with a friend, not your mother. Gerta, she died a few years later, in a camp. But she was my friend at the time; we were in psychoanalytic training together. I think we were coming home from a class. It was a time when Jews had to wear yellow stars and anyone could be stopped on the street." I was scarcely moving, afraid to look at Father directly, but feeling his body beside me and watching him out of the corner of my eye. "Yah, so Gerta and I walked down one of the main streets, I don't remember, maybe Königsbergergasse. Before us, a line of Nazis moved towards us. They were sweeping the crowd for Jews, whom they herded onto the trucks. We both could see it coming. I don't know who thought of it first, or even if we told each other what we would do. But while some people slowed down to show whether they were Christians or Jews, we tore off our yellow stars and kept walking towards the Nazis, and when we met the ring of soldiers we gave them big smiles—like the best of Aryans—and ducked under and went on our way. But the other Jews, the ones who obediently showed the stars on their arms, who knows what happened to them?"

"But you were safe," I said, and looked down at my shoes.

"Yah," he said sadly, as if his safety were not the only point of the story.

"Did you leave Vienna right after that?" I asked, sensing there was something else I might want to know.

"Not right then, but soon." Father pulled his fingers slowly through his hair again. "As soon as I found a way. It was your mother, really, who finally discovered that we might get out as counselors for the children's transport train."

The sky had grown darker, and a long gray cloud hung like a heavy weapon before us. By the edge of the water, Sarah had made a rusty little grocery store from the dead cans, and now she was putting her shoes and socks back on.

"We better go before it starts to rain again," Father said.

"Help me tie my shoes." Sarah looked up at us.

"I'll do it." I bent down and formed careful bows with her brown laces.

I looked up at Father, who was far away behind his glasses. I thought of asking if the rain would give us a sign so we would know when to leave our house, but I said only, "What makes it rain for so many days at a time?"

Father took Sarah's hand, and we turned back towards home. "I don't know."

"What are you thinking about?" I asked after a while, fearful that he might still be recalling Vienna during the Nazis days. I had learned from Father that one could draw a person closer by asking his thoughts.

"What are you thinking about, Daddy? Are you thinking about Vienna?" I repeated, looking up into his gray eyes.

"Hmn? Oh. . . No, I was thinking of a discussion Mordecai and I had yesterday at work. An argument, really."

We were stopped at a corner, and he took off his glasses and wearily wiped his eyes; but then, as if to make things seem ordinary again, he pulled out a handkerchief and began to clean his glasses.

"What was the fight about?" I asked as we started across the street; I felt worried for both him and Mordecai.

"I'm not sure. How we see the role of therapy. But that's not what it was about. It has been building for a long time." Father nodded to himself. "We've both been bruised by the Nazis, only in different ways. So now we fight."

"Did you fight about Lillian?" I worried.

"Yes and no," Father laughed. "Not really. The trouble is old between Mordecai and me."

Father's friendship with Mordecai was the only real one I knew. Mother sometimes talked to the neighbors or to Father's colleagues, but she had no friends. I didn't know why, except that she seemed so nervous and awkward when she was with other people, and she was ready with harsh judgments after they left. I talked to Marilyn Sue in school, only because the teachers had said I should have a school chum. You couldn't call Mrs. Rogers my friend because she was almost Mother's age. Sarah and Bobby Rogers were friends, true. But there had always been something precious between Father and Mordecai. I wondered what I might say to Father to help the two patch up.

"But you ask me why it rains so much." Father rested his hand on my shoulder as we walked.

I waited silently, not sure that I wanted him to return to the problem of the rain. "It's interesting," he nodded rapidly, as if pulling himself away from a daydream. "The water was too high even before the recent rain began. Some areas north of here, in Nebraska and South Dakota, had heavy snow this year."

"We had some snow here too," said Sarah.

"Yah," Father agreed.

"But what makes everything suddenly be too much?" I asked.

$\mathcal{M}$rs. Rogers, a chartreuse scarf wrapped over her pin curls and a man's shirt tied at her thin midriff, stood nervously just inside our front door. I had let her in, and now Mother was coming from the kitchen, wiping her hands.

"Thanks a lot for the cake. Bobby and I really enjoyed it. And I know it's a little late to be asking," said Mrs. Rogers, who suddenly looked around guiltily for somewhere to put out her cigarette.

Mother nodded at me to get an ashtray. "Would you like to sit down?" she said.

"Oh, no thanks," Mrs. Rogers said, glancing over at the living room where Father sat half-reading.

He gave her a nod, as I returned with the ashtray.

"Thanks, hon. Really, I just stopped by, 'cause I thought you'all might want to come along to a picnic. We're having it over at the church, and there'll be music afterwards."

"Mrs. Rogers is in the choir," I proudly informed Mother.

"That's very kind of you," Mother said, and gave a stiff laugh. "I'm afraid I already have dinner almost finished."

"Ma, can't Sarah and I go?" I touched her hand.

"We'll be leaving in about an hour," said Mrs. Rogers, inhaling on her freshly tapped cigarette. Her eyes were darting uneasily at the large painting of the Negro man that hung behind Father. "You don't any of you have to decide now. Just whoever wants to come along, I can honk when I'm ready."

"Please Mommy," I said.

"Well, thank you very much," said Mother. "We will certainly telephone you to let you know."

Father stood from his chair and gave a slight bow as Mrs. Rogers went out.

"Funny, coming outside with her hair in pins." Mother shook her head.

"It would probably be a good experience for the children," Father said.

"I just wish they would go to a synagogue sometimes." She went slowly towards him. "It's confusing for them, if they keep visiting churches."

"We almost never visit churches," I said to Mother. I was following alongside her, waiting for Father's view to win.

"You can take them to a synagogue, if that means something to you," Father pointed out.

Mother didn't look enthusiastic. "We could try lighting candles on a Friday night," she said halfheartedly.

Father shot her a sarcastic look.

"Of course, Mrs. Rogers is probably worried about her husband. She told me when I went over with the cake that he has to have pieces of metal removed from his leg."

"What does that have to do with it?" Father snapped.

"I just thought some of us should give her company." Mother blanched at the sharpness of Father's logic.

"So can I go? Can Sarah and I go?" I asked.

"I have a big meatloaf in the oven, but I guess it can be saved."

I dashed upstairs to tell Sarah, who was happy to go. She also agreed that we should change into the blue and white checked pinafores Mother had sewn us to wear on special occasions. I liked my pinafore especially because it matched the blue rims of my glasses. I placed my hand on my hip and posed like a store window model in front of the mirror.

Half an hour later the air had gotten dark and utterly still, so that you could tell it was going to storm, and Father was reading by lamp light. A bridge near the airport at the east end of town had been knocked out, and the Kaw was covering the highways around Topeka; only one route was left for the mail to enter and leave town. As Mrs. Rogers' car honked, a flash of lightning split open the evening sky. From a distance came the heavy sound of thunder.

"Tell Mrs. Rogers, Thanks again for taking you along," Mother called out as Sarah and I raced down the front steps. Then she stood waving as we got into the car.

Inside the Desoto, the air was thick and sweet with gardenia perfume. Mrs. Rogers had on a bright pink dress, and her long brown hair had been taken out of its pins and combed into the loose curls stylish in the popular magazines that lay on her coffee table. In the rear view mirror, I noticed that she had tweezed her eyebrows until they lay like thin arched shoe laces on her narrow forehead.

"You look nice," I said, excited. Dressed up in church clothes, Mrs. Rogers didn't look like anyone to feel sorry for.

"You girls look real nice too." Through the mirror Mrs. Rogers gave us a lipstick smile to match her dress.

"I got on my new shirt." Bobby twisted in his front seat to show us a starchy collar that cut into his freshly scrubbed neck. His father's army cap covered his rabbit-like face at a tilt.

"How's Mr. Rogers today?" I asked.

"Honey, I haven't heard anything for several days. But, like I told your Mother, it seems they're going to have to operate to take out some of the shrapnel they missed before."

"What's shrapnel?" I asked timidly, leaning forward.

"I don't know, I guess it's pieces of metal from flying bullets—or anything," she said. She kept her eyes on the road ahead, as she fumbled in her handbag for a cigarette.

The darkening evening was dense and muggy as we parked the car down the street from the Church of the Nazarene. A crack appeared in the moody gray sky, and for a moment orange streaks shone out from a high place above the storm where the weather was clear. Then the heavy clouds began to close over the yellow sky.

"I just hope we make it inside with my choir robe," said Mrs. Rogers as she carefully pulled a dress box from the trunk. Then she ran with us toward a vast red tent erected beside the church.

Inside the tent, rows of tables were covered with checked cloths and lined by families leaning over plates piled high with food. The hot greasy odors and noisy crowd reminded me of the fairgrounds. Near the tent entrance, platters of fried chicken, sliced ham, potato salad, colorful green and red jello molds, succotash, macaroni and cheese casseroles, pies with fruit oozing, and luscious frosted cakes, crowded the long table. At the far end, wooden folding chairs had been placed in rows to create an auditorium, and a raised stage with a podium at the side stood ready for the evening's service.

Mrs. Rogers hustled us into the busy food line. Some like us hadn't yet eaten and stood empty-handed, while others held soiled plates waiting for seconds. Mrs. Rogers nervously twirled her key ring; then she fidgeted with Bobby's khaki army cap. "How are you now?" she smiled at friends, her thin face bright and flashy from the special makeup. "How's your husband, dear?" said an old woman with white hair like cotton candy, and touched her hand. We were moving slowly past the tables of people eating. "Purdy new dress," a woman nodded approvingly at her, and Mrs. Rogers smoothed the bright pink linen over her bony hips with her painted fingers. She seemed to know everyone. "These are my neighbor's kids," she would explain, patting my head. I grinned awkwardly, afraid someone would question why we, two Jewish girls, had come to a church party. A tall handsome man with a blond crewcut loped towards us, smiling, and joked with her for a few minutes, and Mrs. Rogers smiled back as glamorously as an actress. Lightning flashed through the tent. Sarah and Bobby were punching each other.

"Don't." I grabbed Sarah's hand.

"I'm not doing anything wrong." She arched her back and giggled at me.

"Be nice, this is a church."

"Church? Church?" She put her fingers over her mouth and snickered. But then she slipped her hand in mine and stood obediently next to me in the line.

We were eating our dinners surrounded by other families when I saw my schoolmate, Marilyn Sue, several tables away. I stopped breathing for a moment, and my heart knocked noisily against my chest. I had tried so hard to make others think we were friends during the school year, but I hadn't thought I would have to see her until school began again in fall. Quickly, I lowered my head and ate with my eyes glued to my plate. But the food tasted dry, like wadded newspaper.

A moment later two small hands covered my eyes.

"Hi!"

"Hi," I said dully, as the saliva drained from my mouth.

I pushed the cool fingers away to see Marilyn Sue grinning down at me. She tossed her dark hair, which had been curled in long old-fashioned ringlets around her heart-shaped face.

"I didn't know you belong to this church," she giggled happily.

"I don't." This was one of the things I didn't like about Marilyn Sue: she could never remember what I'd told her about myself.

"I'm going to sing in the choir when we finish eating," Marilyn Sue chirped, doing a little tap dance by my chair. She had on a white organdy dress with a pink sash.

"So is Mrs. Rogers," I said. "That's who we came with."

Mrs. Rogers had left little bits of food on her plate and was smoking a cigarette. "Hi honey," she said to Marilyn Sue.

"Maybe I should bring over my dessert to eat with you all," suggested Marilyn Sue.

I looked away; the fact that Marilyn Sue didn't take hints was useful in school, where I needed her to stick by me even when I was unfriendly or mean. But now it was June! And I didn't want to see her until September.

"Want to get some cake with me?" she was saying.

"I think the Reverend Thomas is going to call us up to change into our robes very soon." Mrs. Rogers exhaled gray smoke rings over the top of the food-filled table.

"Oh," said Marilyn Sue. "Well, maybe I'll see you after the program."

"I didn't know she was a friend of yours." Mrs. Rogers watched Marilyn Sue skip back towards her own table.

"She's just in my class."

"Sure is a pretty little girl." Mrs. Rogers inhaled dreamily on her cigarette.

Suddenly, with Mrs. Rogers' words hanging in the air, I wished I had been nice to Marilyn Sue. Perhaps I was wrong to dislike her so easily; at this very moment, we could be eating our supper together like regular friends. I searched for her over the rows of seats, and when I found her she was already chatting merrily with someone else.

Mrs. Rogers got up to join the choir, and Sarah, Bobby and I took seats in the rows of chairs facing the stage. A round perspiring woman in a green satin dress sat before an electric organ at the edge of the tent. With strong open chords, she announced a mood of expectant importance. As the last of the people filled the seats, the organ grew brooding and somber.

"Euuu!" Sarah grasped my arm. She looked as if she might cry.

"It's just church music," I consoled her, but I was feeling anxious and unsure about what was to happen.

"It sounds like ghost music," she whispered.

"What? What?" Bobby Rogers floated his fingers eerily in front of her face.

Sarah brushed them aside and grabbed his army cap, which she put on her head. Then she squirmed into a straight position.

Dressed in their purple robes, the choir was filing onto the stage in a snaking line that wove into rows of women on one side of the podium and men on the other. I could see Marilyn Sue in the first row with the other little girls; her mother, a large woman with the same heart-shaped face as Marilyn Sue's, stood near Mrs. Rogers toward the back. I tried to catch Marilyn Sue's attention, but her liquid brown eyes were fastened on a spot at the back of the tent. The organ music suddenly changed again, this time to a bracing opening phrase that ran the length of the keyboard like a high waterfall. A conductor, who had appeared in a black gown between the two groups of purple-gowned singers, beckoned to a young man. He came forward from the line.

> Oh Lord my God,
> When I in awesome wonder

The man's voice was high and clear, like a girl's, and the organ sprayed a waterfall of notes at the end of each phrase.

> Consider all the world
> Thy hands have made.
> I see the stars,
> I hear the roaring thunder.

The organ turned ominous, creating thunder inside the tent.

> Thy power throughout
> The universe displayed.

And now the choir joined in, their voices strong and ardent.

> When Christ shall come
> With shouts of acclamation
> To take me home!

It was as if the moment were here, right now, inside the tent. The ordinary world had backed off and left us free. Electricity whizzed through the air. Someone called "Amen!" Sarah still had on Bobby's hat, but she was gripping my arm again. The music whirled around us, although the choir was only in front. My throat ached to join the singing, but I didn't know the words and was afraid. The soloist had begun a new verse, his voice as smooth and pure as the night. And the choir came forth again, and the conductor motioned to the audience to take part.

> It sings my soul
> my savior come to me
> How great Thou art. . .

Nearly everyone was singing now. I could hear a man's voice behind my head. "How great Thou art," I joined in, fearful but daring, "How great Thou art."

Sounds of relief and happiness splashed about the tent. Without waiting, the choir began a new song, this time more gentle.

> Precious Lord, take my hand
> Lead me on, let me stand,

they sang, and my chest ached, and felt as raw as a scraped knee, against my sundress; and I wanted to sob, without knowing why.

Through the storm, through the night
Lead me on to the light!

Father would shake his head and call the music too
emotional or even trashy. But his eyes might be wet. I wanted to
hold back from the song's power, but I couldn't. I was like a
plant that hadn't drunk water for too long.

Must Jesus bear the cross alone
And all the world go free—

"I spilled something," Sarah whispered, looking down at the
streaks of orange grease on the front of her pinafore.

"How did you do that?" I asked, relieved to be distracted.

"I don't know. Will Mummy be angry?"

"No. She can probably wash it out."

My heart caught as, out of the corner of my eye, I saw a man
in a shiny brown suit leap onto the stage. It was Reverend
Thomas, who stood viewing the choir from the side of the
wooden podium. He seemed to have just stepped from a hot
bath; his skin was pink, and his thin hair lay wet against his
scalp. He had big fleshy lips and darting black eyes.

The song was coming to a close as the choir poured out its
plea.

Take my hand, precious Love,
Take me home.

"I want you to give these people a hand," said the minister,
raising his own large hands in readiness. "We don't usually show
our appreciation, because we're in the house of God. But out
here in the tent, we ought to let them know how great we think
they are, bless the Lord."

All around me, everyone was suddenly clapping. Someone
whistled. I had my cautious eye on the minister, but I clapped
hard. Then I looked at Marilyn Sue, whose tight grin threatened
to break into an irrepressible giggle. Bobby Rogers was slapping
his thighs. He grabbed his army cap from Sarah and threw it into
the air.

"We got people in this choir from nine to practically ninety. Or shouldn't I say how old you folks are—"

And again everyone clapped, and some stamped their feet.

"We're going to pass around a little plate to get the choir some new robes." Reverend Thomas' flashing black eyes grabbed the audience. "I know these people are *hot*, because I've wore their robes. But they don't complain."

A trickle of nervous laughter went through the choir.

The minister suddenly lowered his head and seemed to think deeply. "Paul had in mind, my friends, just what we would have to go through and he made it very plain that we have a great warfare in this world of ours, and I've said it here of late hundreds of times this world is not worth living unless it's lived for the Lord. There's too much trouble, too much misery, too much heartache and pain. Also treachery. Yes treachery and evil, folks. You see it all around you. But when we get to thinking about the Great God of heaven that rules from his heavenly throne, the great Governor of all the earth, and the richness of His promise—"

At that instant, a flash of lightning turned the tent blue-white. For a moment Reverend Thomas stood silhouetted with his arms outstretched. The thunder crashed nearby, and rain began to splash heavily outside the tent. The minister lowered his arms and hunched over dramatically, as if he had been beaten or struck by the great Governor.

Sarah's fingers were digging into my arm. I wished I could leave.

"We are in a time of decision," the minister said quietly. "If the Lord had let me choose, I would have chose to live a long time ago. Yes, I would have chose to live when the first settlers came over across to this country. Because the Lord was with them, friends, the Lord was with them!" As the man's voice became louder, his face too seemed to expand, and his lips were vast and soft like a fish's. "And as they built their log homes, they sang songs of praise to the Lord. And they prayed when they rose up and when they ate their simple breakfast. And they thanked the Lord for what was good. They thanked the Governor of their new land. And the land was rich and good. And they knew that what they had was the *Lord's*, not theirs—that they were just sort of renting it, folks, from the Lord. 'I am weak, but Thou art mighty. Hold me with Thy powerful hands.' They sang songs from the depth of their hearts, just like we've been singing here tonight. And they knew life was no roses. They didn't expect it to be handed to them on a platter, like we do today."

Lightning again blanched the tent, as if it were a flash from a camera. The faces of the choir members glowed a light blue.

What if the bolt itself came down and struck us on the spot? I wondered, hunching into my slatted wooden seat.

"Friends," said the minister, growing more and more excited, "Friends, we are living in a terrible time. People want that silver platter, they want something that the Lord in all His goodness never meant them to have. Colored wants to be white, poor to be rich, woman to be man. They tried to get the colored kids into the white school just back here a week ago," Reverend Thomas pointed accusingly, and his eyes darted at me. "Now was that right? If God had wanted colored folks to be the same as whites, would he have made them separate kinds? Huh? Now you know, does the Lord make mistakes? Does he fool around? Does he?"

"No, sir," said a man in the audience.

Tremors of fear traveled through my body. Reverend Thomas was talking against integration. That was clear! He wanted Mrs. Johnson's boys and Mayella to go to their special school. What he was saying was wrong! But he was making it appear as God's will, and everybody would believe him. I looked to see what Marilyn Sue was thinking, but she seemed to be tickling the girl next to her. Mrs. Rogers and the rest of the choir had turned into statues who looked neither to the right or the left; you couldn't even tell if they were listening.

Reverend Thomas had gone on to make a connection with what was bad about Communists. "Now these people don't believe in the Lord," he was saying. "And they don't believe in the family. Or in work. They want that silver platter, that bed of roses. And when they do get it—which they do, because the Lord is good, and His mercy is infinite—they don't have the sense to bow down and thank the Lord. No, sir! It's a crying shame. They are atheists, every living one of them. That's why I say I wished I had a been allowed to live in an earlier time, my friends." Shaking his head, the man looked as if he would cry, and his thick lips trembled pathetically. "That's why I wished I had been allowed to be born before all this came to pass. But—" He looked up, holding everyone in suspense as he pointed to the roof of the tent. "Friends, I know the Lord Jesus has set me here today to do his very work. And I am grateful to be able to serve the Lord in these hard times. Honored. Humbled. The time is short. We see the waters rising!"

A plate was dropped into my hands, filled with dimes, quarters and dollar bills. I didn't know what to do, and sat tensely, staring at the vast salad of coins and green bills.

"Pass it on," someone whispered.

Relieved, I handed the plate to Sarah, who was nearly dozing. She gave it to Bobby Rogers, who pulled a quarter from his pants pocket.

"What happened before the flood of 1925?" the minister was saying. "People were living easy, high off the hog. Women were smoking in public. Drinking. There was moral depravity, much like now. A mixing of the races. Communism. We've seen it all before! And what happened? Rain. Rain and more rain. But a flood wasn't enough warning. The Lord tries to talk to us, friends, in His way."

"Amen," came a murmur.

"A flood wasn't enough. Because man clings to easy dreams. Oh, man is weak, I'm afraid. Like a baby."

Reverend Thomas seemed to be staring straight at me; his watery black eyes penetrated the raw skin of my face and my thin pinafore. I lowered my eyes, afraid to look back at him. What had I done wrong?

"Now four years after the flood, what happened? It's history, friends! Some of you lived through it—1929! The Great Crash! The Good Lord was saying something to those who'd been deaf and blind."

I glanced up. The minister was now pointing at someone else. He seemed to be making a lot of frightening connections, and his argument reminded me of Lillian's. As if his words had tired them out, Sarah and Bobby were falling asleep. I sat still, glad for the comfort of Sarah's limp body against mine, wishing it were all over and we could go home.

"We still have time, brothers and sisters. God has His Hand on the Kaw, waiting to hear what is in your hearts! There are places where the waters have begun to destroy, I don't need to tell you. But Topeka has been hit lightly so far—compared to other towns around us." The rain made a dull plunking sound as it hit the ground outside the tent. "It's up to you!" the minister pointed, just to my side, making me move quickly toward Sarah. "Look in your hearts tonight. Bible school starts tomorrow. Your children will have the full week to search their tiny hearts for Jesus. The Lord is waiting. I bless you all, for I know most of you, and I don't think you want to live a second without the Lord. God bless you and keep you! And I will personally bless the children that attend Bible school this week." Quickly, he moved to the back of the stage and disappeared into the darkness outside the tent.

The choir began singing a closing hymn. Their words stretched and soared over the night, soothing the nerves the minister had wrought up.

> Je-sus, la-amb of God
> Be mine.

"Amen," said someone.

And it sounded as if someone else were crying softly.

"Be mine."

The choir snaked its way down from the stage, still humming a last hymn. The members pulled off their robes, shaking their bodies free with sighs, to join their families. People were milling about, and the men were already folding tables at the back of the tent. I stood sleepily and stretched. While Mrs. Rogers carefully folded her purple robe, I gave Sarah and Bobby little nudges to wake them up.

$\mathcal{T}$he pungent smells of frying sausage wafted through the air. Was I still at the church picnic? No. We had driven home through driving rain, and Mother had worriedly met us at the door and tucked us quickly into bed. I felt the smooth rim of my sheet, trying to orient myself. Around me charcoal bows threaded their way like long tangled vines over gray walls. I let my eyelids fall shut again, and I could hear the whistling of wind and rain. Then, through my partly opened door, I caught the glimmer of light from downstairs. Throwing off my sheet, I crept down the cool wooden steps to see what was happening.

Though it was wet and dark outside, Father sat at the kitchen table, bent over a plate of black bread, eggs and sausages, the kind of meal he ate only on a leisurely Sunday morning. He looked groggy and tired; and he was wearing the worn clothes he raked leaves in, and giant galoshes.

"What time is it?" I asked, rubbing my eyes.

Mother stood in her loose green bathrobe, without her glasses, watching a pot of coffee on the stove. Her face was still creased from her pillow and her thick hair lay matted at her shoulders. "About two in the morning," she said in a voice that sounded excited and upset.

"What are you doing?"

"Your father has been called to help sandbag the banks along the river." Mother turned from the coffee pot, and her bare eyes were centered in little dots of concern. "The mayor asked for five hundred volunteers. Mr. Cotter just telephoned."

I walked over to the kitchen table and stared down at the yellow half-eaten yolks swimming on Father's plate.

"Why do you have to do that?" I asked.

"The river is breaking through the levees." Father tore off a bite of black bread and began chewing as if he were very hungry. "Your mother explained it quite well: the air force men need to be relieved so that they can get some sleep. I think the area they're worried most about is along the waterworks. That's the most dangerous If the Kaw overflows there, the city loses its drinking water."

I pressed my hand against my forehead; Father's explanation made my head ache. "No, I mean you," I said. "Why did they ask you?" I didn't see how a man used to listening thoughtfully to crazy people in a dim book-lined office could lift sandbags alongside men, like Mr. Cotter, who loaded trucks all day. The way Father was trying to fortify himself by gobbling down his food made him seem particularly inept and wrong for the job.

"They're asking every man. Anyway, Mr. Cotter called me. I'm his neighbor." Father raised his eyebrows and twisted his mouth in attempted humor. "It's a chance to show I'm a useful citizen, don't you think?"

"You don't have to be ironic about helping," Mother admonished.

Father smiled to himself, as he sponged up the runny eggs with his wedge of black bread.

Sliding into a chair sideways to him, I rested my head on my hands. The sounds of organ and choir music from the church picnic were whirling around my mind.

"Efa, *bitte*, you were out very late. It's crazy for you to be up," said Mother, pouring Father his coffee. "*Bitte geh schlafen.*"

I didn't answer, but tried to focus my sleepy mind and concentrate on Father. It wasn't merely that he looked different from other men, he was completely different inside and out. His mind worked more slowly and reached completely unexpected and far out-of-the-way places. He would never go to church like the men who'd moved chairs last night, or like Mr. Cotter did when he drove his family to mass on Sunday. While the other children's fathers dug out vegetable beds for their families or built new playrooms from scratch, Father sat reading his books or playing piano. Or just brooding. I had seen Mr. Cotter gawk at Father when the two were out on the sidewalk and Father thought he had simply been passing time in neighborly talk.

Also, there was his strange throaty accent which I usually couldn't hear but the other men would surely notice.

"I bet you're not strong enough," I warned him.

"They will probably be smart enough to give me work I can do." Father peered at me curiously over his glasses.

"How long are you going to be there?"

"Until the air force men return, or the river falls back, I suppose." I couldn't tell if Father's smirk was aimed at himself or me.

Mother wrapped her arms around his shoulders and nestled her head in his neck. "I'm so glad you were called—so we have a chance to help out like everyone else!"

"I had a very good time last night!" I said to Father, suddenly surging with energy and wanting to distract him with everything I had been too tired to tell him when I came home.

"Efa," said Mother. She straightened up and gave me a hard glance with her bare eyes. "*Bitte!*"

"I'm just talking to Daddy. The music was terrific!" I began, and the suspicion that he would be critical if he heard it made my voice high and excited. "It really was! There was a choir, but even people in the audience knew the songs. Also, they had very good voices!"

Father wiped his mouth, nodding.

"In the synagogue we have a cantor, but no musical instruments," Mother explained.

I winced, and looked up sharply at her. "There was good food too. We should have Jello mold sometime."

"Jello," she shuddered. "Still, you had a wonderful time, despite the terrible weather. That's nice."

"Sort of," I hedged, and turned to Father. "The minister said some funny things."

"What funny things?" He glanced at Mother. "Do I have a rain hat?"

"I'm not sure. I could give you mine." Stretching, she went off to the living room to find it.

"I hope you're not going to wear a lady's hat," I said.

"You'd rather I got my head wet?" he looked amused.

"You're going to look silly!"

"I don't think this is a fashion show."

"Anyway, the minister said the rain was punishment," I said. "He said it was for people wanting the wrong things." I tried to remember carefully. The word integration dangled threateningly before me, but I had seen how upset it made Mother and was afraid to say it. "He said some people wanted to live easier than they should. He mentioned the Communists."

"People say a lot of rubbish these days." Father poured sugar in his coffee and stirred it distractedly with his spoon.

I was beginning to feel dizzy from staying up so long in the middle of the night. Too much was happening, and I couldn't figure it out. I wanted to be upstairs in bed asleep, but I didn't have the strength to get up.

Mother returned with her clear plastic firemen's rain hat. Mr. Cotter stood behind her, broad and pudgy in his delivery man's uniform.

"Look who's here!" she laughed, excited by their adventure.

"You all set?" Mr. Cotter said to Father.

"Can I offer you a cup of coffee before you go?" Mother asked, laying the delicate rain hat on the table for Father.

"Thanks anyway, but my wife fixed me some before I left. Well, I knew this was coming. I coulda told you weeks back!"

Mr. Cotter slapped the thigh of his neatly pressed pants. The man's fat pink face looked pressed out by a cookie cutter; even his voice sounded punched out. Once I'd seen Mr. Cotter chase his two chubby crying children around the backyard. He had made a switch from a green branch and, out of breath, was calling, "Come back here! You come back!" Now his voice was almost raspy. "Half the places on my route, I couldn't even get through to this week. Over in Salina, there was a gosh darn pig on the roof. I don't know if the farmer went and forgot it, or if the animal ran away, or what. But it had crawled up there and was hanging on for dear life, trying to stay dry."

"So you've been living with this for a while." Father took a last swallow of coffee.

"Sure have! I sure have!" The man's small eyes bulged from their sockets.

"I hope you at least can prevent the river from flooding the waterworks. That would be a pity, a city without clean water," Mother shook her head worriedly and touched Father's shoulder.

"We ought to be able to, if we get started," Mr. Cotter nodded. His crew cut was so short you could see the pink crown of his head. "Only thing is, they shoulda built a dike last time this happened."

Father stood up. "Apparently there was opposition, wasn't it you who told me that?" He looked large but drowsy next to Mr. Cotter.

"I don't know, or the government just never got around to building it."

"But we're going to be safe here?" I asked, standing beside Mother. Outside, beyond the window, our yellow reflections mingled with tiny silver slats falling through the black night.

"Oh, yeah, this street is far from the river and way high up. It hasn't never been flooded, I don't think."

"It's quite safe here," Father said, following Mr. Cotter to the living room.

I hung back while Mother said goodbye to Father at the front door. When the men had disappeared into the black rainy night, we stood uselessly about, unsure of what to do. A single table lamp had been lit, and it sent out long yellow streaks onto the shadowy bookcases and the small glass-framed drawings on the wall. The blue Negro man in the painting over the couch watched sorrowfully over the room, and the pink open palm of his hand gave off a comforting glow.

"How long before it gets light?" I yawned. A raw emptiness in my stomach made me want to lie down.

"Two or three hours." With the men gone, all Mother's energy seemed suddenly to have drained away. "We should both go back to bed. We don't help by making ourselves tired and sick."

"Will they be okay?"

"Of course, dearie."

I watched her bend to snap off the light.

"The minister said there was time, if people prayed, to stop the flood from getting worse."

"He seems to have been wrong," Mother yawned, and nodded for me to begin going up the stairs.

"*H*ere's a letter I found on your doorstep. It's a little wet," I said to Mrs. Rogers' narrow face in the large ornately framed mirror the next morning.

She nodded, her mouth tight around bobby pins. She was removing them from the glossy brown coils centered in clear parts, like buttons in the midst of white stitching, all over her head. Even without the pins, her hair hung in silky tendrils from the straight parts. She stood in front of the mirror, her face harsh as she gazed absentmindedly at the dresser top.

"Your hair brush is over there, next to your face cream," I offered.

"Thanks." Mrs. Rogers brushed her hair into wide loops but her face still looked small and sharp, almost ill. "I've got to go to the store for some cigarettes," she said, drawing a thick line of crimson over her lips. As she smeared a little of the extra with her finger to create a blush on her cheeks, she began to look her glamorous self.

"Aren't you going to open your mail?" I fingered the letter at my side.

"When I come back."

"Take an umbrella!" I called as the screen door banged behind her.

I carried the letter into the living room. One of my favorite programs, *Marvel Hill House,* about the trials of an ever-growing foster family, had begun. Mom was looking all over for their newest boy, Jake, who, unknown to everyone in the family, seemed to have gone back to the orphanage, where a sick chum had been left behind. Even Ricky, his new foster brother who hopped around on crutches, was looking all over town. Maybe Mom would have to adopt the chum too—when she discovered what had happened. As the organ music swelled, Mom was holding the phone with tears in her eyes; and you could hear the voice of someone at the agency saying that Jake was there. I wiped my own lids behind my glasses and shook myself.

"Ricky's going to have a leg operation," Mrs. Rogers remarked, as she passed through the living room and set her grocery bag on the kitchen table. "Bobby and your sister still upstairs?" she asked, coming back to the kitchen door.

I nodded yes. They were being so quiet I had forgotten they were there.

"Ricky was really helping to find Jake," I told her.

"What a family!" Mrs. Rogers shook her head and disappeared again into the kitchen. I heard the refrigerator open. "Want a Pepsi?"

"No thanks."

Mom and Ricky were now at the doctor's, and Ricky was kicking and screaming that he didn't want his leg to be operated on. Mom didn't know what to do.

"I ought to pin my hair back up," Mrs. Rogers said, returning with her Pepsi.

I had to pull myself away from the television. "It looks okay to me."

"Yeah, but in this damp weather, it'll be straight by afternoon." Sitting down in the armchair, she reached for the box of bobby pins, mirror and comb she kept on the end table.

Mom still had to pick up Jake from the orphanage, but she couldn't just leave Ricky with the doctor. She got on the telephone to tell Pop to come over to the doctor's office.

Mrs. Rogers was tying a silk scarf around her pin curls when the commercial came on again. "They don't tell you on the TV that most of the kids you get that way are colored," she said.

"How do you know?" I turned to her.

"I was going to adopt a kid one time."

"Really?"

"Two years ago. Lee was over in Korea, just like he is now, and I decided I wanted a baby girl. For company, you know. Bobby was getting so ornery you couldn't hardly talk to him."

I wondered what it would have been like with a little Negro girl on our street, but I was afraid to express the idea aloud for fear Mrs. Rogers would talk like Reverend Thomas. "Why didn't you do it?" I cautiously asked.

"Honey, like I told you, they were nearly all colored babies."

"But you still could have."

"What are you saying?"

"Why not?"

"What am I going to do with a little colored kid? You just wouldn't want to."

"Is it because of some of the things Reverend Thomas said?" I asked, now more afraid not to know how Mrs. Rogers stood on these cloaked and confusing matters.

She gave me an impatient look.

"You know, about integration."

"He's just saying people should be happy with who they are, and not to try to be anyone else. It's what Jesus says. It's even in your Ten Commandments," she looked pointedly at me.

"People could be happy to be themselves and still want to be friends with other kinds of people," I said, feeling a mysterious compulsion to speak like my mother.

"Friends maybe. Except it's hard to be friends with people who have different ways."

"But babies would grow up in your house. Anyway, people aren't so different inside." This sounded so much like my mother that I felt ashamed.

"Eva," she said crossly. "I don't want to adopt no colored baby. Anyway, where is that letter you brought in?"

I pointed to the top of the television set.

Mrs. Rogers lit a cigarette and reached for the envelope. I watched her rip it open with her long red fingernails. "Cripes," she said, and inhaled deeply.

I could see it was a short typed letter.

"Jesus," she said.

A new program had come on that I didn't care much about. Mrs. Rogers' long face had turned greenish, and her jaw was working in a strange way. "Do you want me to go home?" I asked, not knowing whether to comfort her or leave her alone.

"Leave canceled on account of medical complications." She sucked deeply on her cigarette. "Says something. . . I guess something happened when they tried to take the shrapnel out."

"Is the shrapnel still in his leg?"

"Oh, shit! How should I know? Why didn't he write and tell me himself? I was hoping he'd be home for the Fourth." Her face was suddenly striped with red.

I stood uneasily, feeling I should leave.

"Bobby'll sure be disappointed. He was expecting his dad to be home to set off the fireworks," Mrs. Rogers said unsurely, sniffing.

"Maybe we could have the fireworks at our house this year," I suggested.

"Yeah, I suppose so."

"What a day! First the river, and then—all this!"

"Well, we can't do nothing about any of it, except maybe pray, I guess." Mrs. Rogers snuffed out her cigarette and lit another. She picked up her crocheting and began to work mechanically with her eyes fixed on the screen.

I was still standing by my chair, one foot crossed over the other, when she said, "Eva, why don't you go check on what Bobby and Sarah are doing."

"I was thinking of going home," I said.

"Well, that's fine then, if that's what you want."

A minute later, I was scampering up the steps to my house, relieved by the chance to be back in my own life. My house would be airy; Mrs. Rogers' curtains were drawn for the TV, and she didn't even see the rainy days.

Inside my living room, I was surprised to find Mrs. Johnson sitting properly on the couch in her travel clothes, while Helene, who never came over in the daytime, sat, long legs sprawling before her, facing Mrs. Johnson, with her back to the front door. Closing the screen door quietly, I stood at the piano.

"Do your children ever talk about what the white schools seem like to them?" Helene was saying. She had on a wide flowered skirt and string sandals, and her hair was cut straight in back.

"Well, of course they can't help notice that the schools are bigger and newer and have all those playgrounds with special jungle gyms and swings and things. But I don't think they pay them too much attention."

"But what do you think it makes them feel, not having all that good new equipment?"

Mrs. Johnson shook her dark head in rapid spurts. "I guess it don't make them feel very good," she said. She gave me a quick nod, and patiently folded her hands.

"Like they don't deserve as much as the white children?"

"I don't think they think like that."

"And what if their schools were fixed up to be as good, but they still had their own separate schools?"

"What, they gonna do that for us?" Mrs. Johnson looked skeptical. "Anyhow, we gonna give the white folks some disease?"

"That's how it would make you feel?"

"If we were the ones to decide about being separate. But you know who's going to say whether we'll be separate or together." Mrs. Johnson said, and looked at her hands.

"Hi," I finally decided to announce myself, and Helene turned to me.

"Hi, kiddo."

"Where's everyone?"

"Your father just came back from the river and is resting and talking to your mother upstairs. I'm speaking to Mrs. Johnson."

"Can I listen?"

"If Mrs. Johnson doesn't mind."

"Eva can listen to whatever she wants," Mrs. Johnson said gruffly. "She's always worrying about these things."

Carefully, I went over and sat on the far side of the couch. Though I didn't understand exactly what they were talking about, I sensed something important was going on. I glanced over at Mrs. Johnson, who was now speaking with disgust about the torn old books her children had to use. Crossing my hands in imitation of hers, I looked up at Helene. Now that I was facing her, I could see she was scribbling notes on a pad that lay on her full skirt. Her bent face looked serene as she listened and wrote intently.

"Anyway, no one's going to make me believe they'd build a new school like the white one, fill it with new equipment, and just give it to us," Mrs. Johnson was saying.

J reached the dissonant last note of a Bartok exercise and with relief unstuck the cumbersome violin from my chin.

"Pretty good," said Father, who sat next to me at the piano in his open-necked shirt that showed the dark hairs of his chest. His nose was red, and he was still sneezing from having caught a cold at the waterworks. "You begin to get the feel of Bartok, no?"

"Mm."

I shuffled my sheets of music until I came to the Palestrina piece and lifted my violin back onto my shoulder. The man's name sounded like Palestine, the land where Mother had wanted to go. Though Mother said the country was bursting with orange trees from the valiant efforts of our people, the music harkened back to a flat desert without palms and no cheery sun. Placing my bow across the strings, I waited for Father's nod to begin. My fingers moved up and down the clef, while I ran my bow carefully back and forth in dismal time. The piece was somber, without spirit, like the march of tired old men who could barely pick up their feet. Even the little half notes had no lightness about them. They ought to have been played by a tuba, not a violin. After a few minutes, I let the notes move directly from the page to my fingers and freed my mind to wander back to the morning of television in Mrs. Rogers' darkened living room and Helene's talk with Mrs. Johnson. It was awful about Mrs. Rogers' husband, and I wasn't sure whether she had wanted to adopt or take a foster child. I tried to remember what she'd said Jesus thought we ought to do. It hadn't sounded as bad as Reverend Thomas. But it wasn't at all the same as the way Mrs.

Johnson and Helene were talking. Although Mrs. Johnson hadn't said so, I could tell she wanted her children to come to school with us.

My violin had grown heavy and an ache was beginning to spread from my perspiring neck outward along the top of my arm. I leaned the tip of the violin against the piano's music ledge. I should have stood up straight and balanced the instrument properly, but even with my three-quarter size violin it took so much will to fight the strain.

Father nodded to and fro in time to the barren dirge, and his dark hair drooped curtain-like over his face. Yet I knew that from behind the double screen of hair and glasses, he kept track of each note, holding it with utter accuracy until the instant it demanded to be released. He had already caught me on several mistakes, and each time his voice had rung out far more harshly than when Mrs. Johnson had finally complained that there were no running toilets at her children's school.

Outside, Sarah's high voice pierced the air as she tore across the front lawn with Bobby Rogers. It was drizzling a little, but not enough for Mother to call them in.

"Eva, if you're so tired, maybe you better practice after supper." Father's reprimand cut into my ruminations and the heavy notes of Palestrina.

The last thing I wanted was to start all over after dinner! Which, in any case, was when he had promised to go for fireworks. "I can't see the music," I lied, stopping to shift my glasses on my nose.

Father pushed the sheet in my direction. "Come, start back again from the new phrase," he directed.

I had just lifted my violin cleanly to my chin, ready to take on the burden of correct posture, but now I dropped the instrument in disgust.

"Here. Come." He thumped the page.

"I hate this piece!"

"Just from here to the end. Then we'll play something that you like."

"Get Sarah to learn an instrument, if you like this kind of music so much," I dared him, though the choice of Palestrina was actually my teacher's, Miss Rideaux's.

"Look, there are lovely sections." He leaned into his trusty piano and ran his strong fingers easily over the ivory keys. After being out all night, he looked tired but normal, not much different, it seemed, than after any day of work. And the music *was* lovely—when it came from his fingers. Perhaps he played it more rapidly than I; certainly he gave it a smoother, more energetic flow. To encourage him, I stood over his shoulder with my eyes glued to the little notes that marched past on the page. Maybe he would forget himself and play to the end of the composition. From the kitchen came the clang of Mother dropping a fork or spoon. We were to have scalloped potatoes for supper, and the soft milky aroma was beginning to thicken the air.

Father finished the last stately notes of the movement. "See what you just played?"

"It's nice."

He rested his firm but fine hands on the piano ledge. "Now try again."

After dinner, I went upstairs and took my piggybank from my bookcase. Sitting on my bed, I unplugged its belly and let its insides spill out. Last year, Mr. Rogers had been home on leave for the Fourth of July, and I hadn't even thought of where Mrs. Johnson's children went to school. As the sky darkened, he had stood in his crisp uniform in the middle of their backyard and set off one display after another. There were fireworks that shot into the air like rockets in stages, ones that sprayed out into brightly colored fans, and ones that spurted in a series of patterned stars. Afterwards, Mrs. Rogers had brought out little cups of straw-berry ice cream. Did the Johnsons set off fireworks, and what did they have to eat? By the time we had come back across the street, Mother and Father had been waiting to turn out the lights and go to bed. This year, despite all my announcements about the upcoming holiday, Father had held off buying fireworks. Although I had finally gotten him to agree to take us to the stand, he would never be as generous as Mr. Rogers. Even if I used every penny, I had only eighty cents. Yet I was intent on having as good a display as last year. Looking at my neat stacks, I swept my hand over them and once more mixed up the coins.

"How much do you think a really nice fireworks display would cost?" I said to Father, beginning slowly as he drove Sarah, Bobby Rogers and me out toward the south side of town, away from the river.

"For me, the best way to celebrate the Fourth of July would be for us all to read a little history," Father said gruffly.

"Daddy!"

"Do you even know what the holiday commemorates?"

I was certain that he was being unfair. "I wish you had seen Mr. Rogers' display last year, because I mean like that." I turned to Bobby. "How much do you think your father spent?"

"I don't know." Bobby was staring quietly out the back window. He was still out of sorts from the news of his father.

"Well, your dad did a great job, because I still remember," I told him. "Most parents buy fireworks for their children," I turned to Father. To me, it was suddenly clear that through fireworks, even if not through Jesus, we could save ourselves. "Actually, I think all. Anyway, everyone knows about the Fourth of July—Boston Tea Party and the American revolution."

"Revolution? Is that what they call it in your school?" Father laughed sarcastically.

"Mr. Cotter bought some today," Sarah came to my aid, leaning over the front seat.

We drove past the Veterans Administration Hospital. Low brick buildings and Quonset huts filled block after block in strict rectangular rows. Picking up Father on afternoons when he visited mental patients there, I had seen soldiers from World War II who had stumps for legs or were missing arms, and some were a little crazy. Once Father had gone especially to talk to a man who had tortured people in the War and couldn't find peace. Perhaps Mr. Rogers would be sent there when he finally came home.

The little fireworks stand had been decorated with red, white and blue stripes, and the proprietor was a heavy tired woman in a vast print apron. Though the stand was supposed to look festive, rain had bled the stripes and the stand looked more like a rundown chicken coop in a sea of mud.

Father blew his nose. "Not so much business with the rain and the flooding," he said to the woman. At least he was trying to be friendly!

"Oh, it ain't too bad," she answered. Her yellow teeth were hollowed out by black cavities, as if she never went to the dentist. "Most folks still want something, and of course they couldn't set up their stands over on the north side this year, so the people come here. Most folks still do want something." She dug her hands in her faded coin-filled apron pocket.

I looked at a little round package covered with blue stars; it promised to send up a spray of different colored meteors. The trouble was, if I bought it, I would scarcely have enough money for the sparklers. With each dime turning into only a few seconds of light or sound, I didn't see how I could stretch my money into the rich display Mr. Rogers had created. I handed the little package to Father, hoping he would be enticed into contributing some money.

Father read the inscription, then laid the package back on the display counter. "If it rains, you won't be able to use that at all."

I picked it up again. "It's not going to rain."

"I wouldn't count on that," he smiled.

"Anyway, don't you think it would be pretty?"

"Not particularly."

"Then what should I get?"

"I'm buying my own sparklers," Sarah decided.

"But if you get that," I cried, "we won't be able to buy anything else!"

"I want sparklers. And bangers," Sarah smiled coyly at Father and the woman. She was always most winsome when she was trying to defy me and go her own way.

"Sarah!"

"Eva, you haven't even begun to spend your own money," said Father.

"This here, Niagara Falls, is kinda nice." The woman's fingers were ridged with dirt as she handed me a red and white package that looked like an ice cream cone.

I tried to concentrate on the cone and imagine its pink and white sprays, then passed it to Father.

He examined the package critically. "You're going to waste twenty-five cents when it doesn't go off. This is one of the most expensive kinds." He began to whistle the Palestrina we had played, and a fine rain started to fall.

Bobby Rogers was methodically filling his frail arms with little packages.

"What about this?" I showed Father one that Bobby had left behind.

"I don't know," he shrugged, still whistling.

"Then what are we supposed to get?" I yelled.

"Eva, calm yourself."

I threw down my sparklers, "I'm not buying anything!" and tramped through the muddy lot to the car. My eyes blurred with sudden tears as I slammed the door. Outside the dripping window, Sarah, Bobby and Father were busily working out their purchases by the fireworks stand. Why! Why! Why! I whispered in a watery haze. Nothing. Not my father, not the world. Nothing at all seemed fair.

Sarah held a bag triumphantly in her chubby hand as she came skipping toward the car. Half hidden by his big army cap, Bobby was walking obediently next to Father; the two talked quietly, man to man.

"Everything I got we can use on the front porch!" Sarah grinned happily at her successful compromises as she squeezed into the back seat. She pulled out a package of sparklers, carefully closing the sack after herself.

"What kind of sparklers?" I asked impatiently.

"Pink."

"I got silver," said Bobby, peering into his bag."

Father slid into the driver's side and inserted his key in the ignition. Then he pulled out a handkerchief and blew his nose. "Eva, you owe me fifty cents," he said without looking at me.

"I didn't choose anything."

I could feel his harsh glance. "You know, the rain has caused floods that destroy people's businesses and homes."

"And Helene's working to save the schools for Mrs. Johnson's children," I shot back.

"Well, so try to get a little perspective on what's important."

"Anyway, I thought we were doing this for Bobby, because of his Father being away," I returned, sickened by my own failure.

Father shrugged. "You didn't help there much either."

It rained all day on the Fourth, and I stayed in my room reading *The Secret Garden*. Looking out the window in the evening, I could see Mr. Cotter trying unsuccessfully to set off a few firecrackers while his children stood gloomily around him. The ground was too wet. Sarah, Bobby, and I had our sedate celebration, ending with chocolate chip cookies, out on our front porch. Thanks to Bobby Rogers, a sullen truce seemed to have been declared: Mother and Father didn't mention either the rain or the reasons why America wasn't exactly the place to celebrate, and I didn't complain about the meager display. But the next morning Mother showed me the newspaper heading: "Fourth of July Tragedy Hits North Topeka Family." In a fuzzy photograph the tip of a house peered out at a slant from a sink hole that had suddenly opened like a canyon. A day later other sink holes appeared. The paper said the sink holes were caused either by quick sand or saturation from overflowing sewers. The Mayor was declaring a state of emergency in Topeka, and the Governor was flying to Washington to ask for federal aid.

*T*hat summer, life seemed to grow as upset inside the house as the weather outside. One day, book in hand, I came galloping down the stairs as I heard Father's angry voice. When I reached the bottom step, Mother swept me inside the kitchen and closed the swinging door.

"What's happening?" I asked.

"Your father is on the telephone."

"I know. Who's he talking to?"

"Mordecai, I think."

I perched myself on the red kitchen stool. Mother was intently doing hand wash in the sink, and the splashing of water as she mashed the clothes interfered with the clarity of Father's words. Still, his voice as it penetrated the dining room door was harsh with fury. I slid off the stool.

"Stay out of the living room," Mother warned.

"The telephone is in the dining room." My hand was on the white enameled door.

"Don't be cheeky. You know what I mean."

I went out of the door and settled myself on the piano bench, my book at my side. I was at the far end of the living room, out of Father's sight.

"That's pure insolence!" Father was shouting. I imagined him pacing before the large bay window where Mother kept a green profusion of indoor plants. Sometimes Father talked comfortingly on the telephone to patients who called him because they were too confused or afraid to wait until their next appointment. But I had never heard him have a fight on the phone. And with Mordecai! "It certainly *is* insolent!" Father repeated, still angrier.

I studied a page of Mahler's *Kinder Totenlieder* Father had opened on the music rack—it was gloomy, soul-stirring music—but my attention was suspended in wait.

"Now just hold it a minute.—*Ein* moment!—*Nein!*" In his rage, he was reverting to German, which I'd never heard him speak with Mordecai. "*Warte nur!* Just wait a minute, give me a chance, will you!" His voice was so loud that Mordecai had to be yelling. "Oh, perfect. Just perfect. Thanks to David Hoffman, psychoanalysis becomes available to every fool and bigot—free of charge, of course! Their character armors dissolve, like dirt under one of those American miracle cleansers, wouldn't you say? And fascism becomes impossible, not just in America, but on this planet!" Father thumped something, perhaps the dining room table, with his fist. "It's the Communist Youth Group all over again," he gave a mean laugh.

"Afraid? I don't think so. Okay, disillusioned, and I exaggerate, for the purpose—"

Now Mordecai seemed to be developing his side of the argument, for Father was silent, though I could hear his leather soles squeaking against the wooden floor as he paced restlessly up and down, back and forth. He must be walking the length of the dining room table, stretching the coils of the telephone wire at each end.

"Oh, I'll take your example!" he appeared to break in. "What? No. Let's say I put our noble Superintendent of Schools, or perhaps our fine Senator, on the couch three times a week for five years. You'd like that, eh? 'Did you have any nice dreams last night?' What a pleasant time I'll have. And what happens if—it's a mere possibility, you have to admit it—what if psychoanalysis merely frees their inhibitions so that they become less neurotic, more efficient at their grisly—" Mordecai had apparently intervened. "It's a possibility, you know." I looked at the score before me, following its unhappy line of thought by sounding out the German words.

> *Nun will die Sonn' so hell aufgeh'n*
> *Als sei kein Unglück, die Nacht gescheh'n!*
> *Das Unglück geschah nur mir allein!*

> Now the sun will rise as brightly
> as if no bad luck had occurred in the night.
> The bad luck fell on me alone.

"Oh no you can't," interrupted Father. "You can't have it both ways. Certainly not! You're under the illusion that everyone becomes a better person. It's your initial premise; it always has been. You also think everyone's good at bottom. Decent. Isn't it capitalism, or repression, that causes all the trouble?—Ha!—Okay.—Yah.—Okay." And his voice seemed calmer, not as angry. Maybe Mordecai had kidded him.

> *Du musst nicht die Nacht in dir verschränken,*
> You must not let the night enclose you;

The song was about a man who loses his two children to scarlet fever, Father had explained. When he sang it, his jaw wobbled and his eyes glazed.

> *Musst sie ins ew'ge Licht versenken!*
> You must sink in the eternal light.

"No, it's silly on the telephone." I wished I could go into the dining room to tell Father to say hello to Mordecai from me. "Look, here's a joke, and then I should get off," Father was saying. "A minister comes before the House on Un-American Activities. Someone asks McCarthy about what the man can possibly have done wrong. He's a minister, after all." I let out a relieved breath at Father beginning to joke; it meant he wanted to soften things between himself and Mordecai. "'The man is a subversive,' insists McCarthy—Naturally. 'You know what our committee found him telling his congregation? The poor shall inherit the earth!'" Father gave a bitter laugh and knocked, though this time it sounded more like the crack of the wall against his fist. The joke wasn't as friendly as I had wished.

"What?—No, go ahead if you have the conviction. I know what Helene's doing. I envy you both."

Mordecai must have been explaining or arguing, for once again Father was silent. Then, "Okay, okay, you're right," he said. "Okay, *auf wiedersehen*, so long."

I heard the click of the phone and Father stood quietly where he was. When I heard his nearing footstep, I thought of disappearing upstairs. I could feel him coming towards me across the length of the living room and then he settled down on the piano bench in front of the lower registers.

"You're practicing Mahler?" he asked, though the arrangement was for voice and piano.

I looked silently at the music.

"Get out your violin and play the voice line," he instructed and, adjusting his glasses, set his fingers to the keys.

S arah and I were upstairs, drying ourselves off from our baths, when the doorbell rang. I could hear Mother welcoming Hans and Anna Mandelbaum. Then the women's voices faded—they had probably gone into the kitchen—while the men continued talking to each other. Hans' violin, so much richer and more vibrant in tone than mine, began to be tuned to Father's piano. Hans and Father would play a phrase, reminding each other of a piece they might try, then say a few words about their patients to each other. Hans' thick German accent came out as deep and raspy as his violin was high and sweet. Despite a slight hoarseness from his lingering cold, Father's voice still seemed comfortably middling, like the notes he played on the piano.

"Let's start with a duet while we're waiting for Micha," I heard Father suggest. I was standing in the upstairs hallway, tying my blue cotton bathrobe around my waist. I could feel my hair wet against my neck. I went back into the bathroom, where Sarah stood on her toes at the sink, brushing her teeth before the mirror.

"You're getting Mrs. Johnson's mirror all full of toothpaste," I said, pulling a towel off the rack. "Aren't you going to eat dessert with company?"

"Ooops, I forgot!" Sarah shook out her toothbrush.

The rich melancholy sounds of a Mozart duet floated up from downstairs.

"I don't like that stupid Mrs. Mandelbaum," Sarah grimaced. "She's icky."

"She's a little crazy, because the whole family spent the war crouched in a chicken coop," I reminded Sarah. In Holland, a farmer had brought them potatoes each day; only on dark nights could they go outside to stand up straight. Now their son Bruno, who was never sure he would have enough to eat, stole bread from the table.

"I don't care, she's still icky."

I rubbed my hair hard with the towel. A hot decayed smell came from Mrs. Mandelbaum's mouth: you couldn't like her, even though you knew she'd had such a bad time. "The worst thing, she doesn't smell good," I confided guiltily to Sarah.

The music stopped as the doorbell rang again. Micha was saying, "Hallo! Hallo!" in her throaty Hungarian. I would have liked to see Janosh, her painter husband who winter and summer wore a red scarf at his neck, but I didn't hear his voice. Then Micha's cello case snapped open, and the deep mellow notes of her instrument wafted up to us as she began to tune.

"Micha's not icky." Sarah gazed up at me.

"I know, but she's also a little strange." I wasn't sure why I had said that, except that she went most places without her husband, which Mother would never do. And once, chatting with me, she had suddenly unwound her long black braids from their heavy coil at the back of her head. I had been able to do nothing but stare, for with her thick brows and her hair flowing like a dark river to her waist, she had seemed like a dangerous creature, part mermaid part horse.

"I hope Mrs. Mandelbaum doesn't try to kiss me," Sarah giggled as we crept down the stairs. The musicians were playing a strangely dissonant and wistful piece that swept in and around the spaces between the walls and filled the house. I would have said it was Schumann, if Father had asked me to guess.

"You'd better be nice," I whispered.

We sat at the bottom of the stairs, nestled against the white railing slats. Facing us at the far end of the living room were Mother and Mrs. Mandelbaum, who sat quietly on the couch with their stockinged legs neatly crossed in honor of the private concert. Mother had on a pretty brown dress and was smocking a white blouse with colored threads for Sarah. But Mrs. Mandelbaum, who had shut her eyes to concentrate on the music, wore a gray silk, patterned like something Grandmother would have worn, and her breasts seemed shrunken behind the loose bodice. Above them, the Negro man rested his bony head thoughtfully in his pink palm, contemplating the odd little gathering of foreigners.

Father's back was turned to the room as he leaned toward the piano and ran his hands over the keys in a lurking, cautious melody. Behind him sat Hans and Micha, who had propped yellowed music sheets on the spindled metal racks before them. Although Hans was Father's age, the few hairs on his head were gray and soft, like used tufts of cotton. His long back was permanently stooped from his years in the chicken coop, and, as he took up the melody on his violin, he swooped and swayed like a listing sailboat. Two dark furrows lined Micha's forehead; she was drawing her bow across the strings in a haunting sound. A fringed crimson scarf draped over her bright patterned sundress. With her black hair and dark skin, she looked more like a gypsy than a psychiatrist.

The music made me think of a dark woods, and an animal, perhaps a deer, out alone without a place to stay. The music dipped and swelled as the animal searched for a home. There seemed so much loneliness in the world! I glanced at Father. A tear glistened on his unshaven cheek. Father never cried, except to the beauty of music, and the sight of his tears sucked the breath from my lungs. Maybe tonight he was thinking of Mordecai. Was he wishing he had sounded less harsh? The cello played a mournful solo, like a call from an untamed place where beings could cry out openly whatever they needed. Hans had rested his violin on his lap, but his lean head nodded dolefully to the cello's sounds. Tears were still glazing Father's cheeks when he joined the cello in a new duet of something like anger or strength. Then Hans lifted his violin, and, as the piece swooped to a close, the three sounded like thoughtful birds who had reflected on the pain of the world.

"*Ach*!" Father sighed, and turned his wet cheeks towards his partners.

"Bravo! Bravo!" Mother called from the green couch. Mrs. Mandelbaum tilted her head and clapped weakly. She had puffy bruises under her eyes.

"It's good." Hans wiped the perspiration from his wrinkled forehead with a soggy handkerchief.

"Hallo Eva! Hallo Sarah!" Micha looked up at us for the first time, and her black eyes were piercing but friendly. She squirmed in her seat to adjust the cello between her legs. Under the shadow of her print dress, I could see the ends of her stockings cutting into her heavy thighs.

"Hi," I bit my lip.

"Hi," said Sarah, standing up.

"Let's play another before we stop," Father suggested to Micha and Hans. "Okay?" he smiled at Sarah and me quizzically, then turned towards his group. "Let's try the Brahms piano trio." He rummaged through his music and brought down a score from the piano top.

"*Ach, Gott!* It's raining outside," Mother sighed from the couch. She put away her needlework and went to the window.

"Already five cases of polio this week reported in the newspaper," Mrs. Mandelbaum muttered worriedly to herself.

"There's nothing we can do now." Micha nodded at Father. Then she laid her bow decisively across the strings.

On the piano, Father began a call like a man whistling as he walked over a wide field, and Hans repeated the phrase with his violin. Then Micha came in with the same contented refrain. The composition was a gentle braid of the three instruments playing off each other. Usually the piece would have swept me in, but I was watching Mother at the window. Each day now, the flood was making her more agitated. She had even fretted to me in the afternoon that Father ought to cancel his chamber music evening. With hundreds of families threatened daily with flooding, she thought that the only decent thing was to pour her attention single-mindedly onto their lives and the treacherous river.

Sarah got up from the steps and disappeared into the kitchen, only to return a minute later with a fistful of pinwheel cookies.

"Want one?" she grinned.

I followed her up the stairs so that Mother wouldn't see us eating them. We settled on the little Persian carpet on the landing, just hidden from view. The cookies were still warm and smelled of fresh eggs and sugar. I nibbled around the circle, limiting my taste first to the heavy sweet chocolate and then to the smooth vanilla. The sounds of Brahms filled the snug little landing. Not being able to see the players made it almost like listening to a record or the radio—except that I could still picture the way Father, Micha and Hans swayed together in rhythm to the melody. Maybe Father was crying again; I couldn't tell from the music. The trio was strong and vigorous now, with only threads of wistfulness here and there. When we finished our cookies. Sarah returned to the bottom of the stairs. I watched her go and then sat with my eyes closed in the corner of the landing.

The piano seemed to be insisting or pointing out something to the other instruments. The violin and the piano grew gentle together, then turned forceful again. The cello and the violin returned to the beginning refrain that had reminded me of walking over a field. Only now something made me think of looking over the flooding of a small town from the distance of an airplane or a high hill—like in the newspaper photographs that had made everything seem less urgent, even peaceful. There was strength and sadness, but humor too.

I could hear the clinking of dishes in the kitchen. Mother must have begun to prepare the coffee and arrange the sweets on a tray. If I went downstairs now, I could help her serve. But Sarah was probably already bringing out the coffee cups. Anyway, it seemed nicer to join the adults when the music had stopped and they were all sitting around the coffee table.

Father was humming along with his "na na na" half-talking voice. I climbed down to sit at the bottom of the steps for the remainder of the trio. The violin and cello were again repeating the beginning refrain, but this time with passion, while the piano galloped beneath them. Micha shook her head to the music, and her forehead was lined with deep furrows of concentration. Little beads of sweet lay on Hans' wrinkled forehead. I could sense them coming to an end as they played vigorously together, then went off on little quiet tangents, and finally joined their melodies—at the same moment.

The three turned gratefully to each other.

"Nice," breathed Father. His face looked relaxed and satisfied.

"I always love that." Micha shook her head rhythmically, as if continuing the trio in her inner ear.

"Coffee!" Mother called from the kitchen door with nervous gaiety.

"We should stop and have coffee now," Father nodded.

"After coffee, we must let Eva play with us." Micha winked at me.

"Yah, we can find something simple," agreed Father.

"Give her a second violin part. You can play viola on the piano."

"You want to try?" he asked me, and turned to look through his sheet music for the quartets.

"Maybe, if it's not too hard," I said quietly, my heart leaping.

Micha and Hans leaned their instruments against their open cases and headed for the couch and chairs.

"What a pity the people whose houses are full of water can't at least hear this beautiful music," Mother sighed as she brought the coffee to the table.

"They probably have more important things to do," chuckled Micha.

"True. But it would give them a lift, such beautiful music," Mother insisted weakly. "Don't you think?" She turned to Anna Mandelbaum.

"The music was quite nice."

This weak response seemed to give mother courage. "David was out with the other men from town, helping on the dikes," she said brightly, looking around the room.

"Yah, you were?" said Micha. "I talked to Mordecai. He said he was there too, but he didn't mention you."

"I went with a neighbor," Father said quietly, and his face seemed to gray for an instant.

Micha gave her throaty laugh. "Mordecai was apparently somewhere along the river with a couple of the older refugees from the   ic. He said he heard, '*Bitte Herr Doktor.*' '*Danke Herr Doktor.*' '*Bitte Herr Doktor.*' '*Danke Herr Doktor.*' as they passed the bags all the way up and down the line."

Father chuckled.

"*Ach*, those people still want to be in Europe," said Mother, with disgust. Thinking about the older refugees at Menninger's always made her feel that she'd quickly become a real American.

Hans stuffed his handkerchief into his pocket and stood looking over the tray of cakes. "But flooding makes some of my patients real crazy!"

"It's good for the fear of the Mother," Micha laughed.

I got up from the stairs. "How's Lillian?" I asked.

Hans turned to me with curious hollow eyes. "You know Lillian?"

"Yes, I talk to her when I come to pick up Daddy at the clinic." I neared the coffee table.

"Well, in the rain she got a little crazier. There was nothing I could do. Vush! Every day we had to call the plumber, she stuffed so much clothes down the toilet!"

"I heard she's in the locked ward now." Micha helped herself to *butterkuchen*.

Hans nodded. "Yah, she's not dangerous, but she makes everywhere such a mess."

A dark wire screen enclosed the porch where the locked-ward patients got their fresh air. Sometimes strange sounds came from the shadowy figures. Once I stood below as a man sang the famous Carmen song in a beautiful baritone; each note was perfect, except that they were all even, as if sung to a metronome. Would Lillian feel angry or afraid behind the screen? Father was standing by the coffee table and looked as if he were about to add something sarcastic, but nothing seemed to come out and he stood nodding sheepishly.

"Take a piece of cake, you should take a piece of cake," Mrs. Mandelbaum instructed her husband, who still stood motionless over the food. She had placed her own small slice of *butterkuchen* in an odd way, at the very edge of her plate.

Sarah helped herself to more pinwheel cookies. Grinning, she held up her bulging hands for me to admire.

"It's not fair. Imagine, here we are, dry and safe, with good food and beautiful music, while so many people have their homes and crops destroyed." Mother was still worrying about all the people outside the room.

"Leah, you're so good," Micha sighed impatiently.

"Leah identifies with all refugees," Father noted gruffly.

"*Ach*," Mother sighed, looking hurt.

"You know, the flood is making the polio worse this year," Mrs. Mandelbaum repeated her worry in a clipped staccato voice. She was picking at her cake like a bird nipping at seed.

"You have to keep Bruno cool and away from dirty water," said Mother, suddenly back into the conversation. "Of course, now we will have the typhoid to worry about too."

"Eie yie yie! What do we do with typhoid?"

"You can get shots, which might be a good precaution. My children have them already."

Micha waved at them as she chewed her cake. "Please, the two of you! We're having a nice evening with good music and fine pastry!"

Mother looked as if she might cry. "You're right, you're right," she apologized, serving herself a shaky slice of *butterkuchen*. "Take some, everybody," she demanded with forced cheer. "I made so much. This isn't a good time to waste."

"You can take whatever we don't eat to the refugees," Father teased.

Micha raised her eyebrows at Father; she knew he was usually more gentle with Mother, especially in front of company. "You heard, I suppose. Helene testified at the school segregation case the other day."

"I heard she was good," Father said, "but that unfortunately they lost the case."

"She talked to Mrs. Johnson at our house," I told Micha.

Micha nodded at me. "Helene says they lost, but in a useful way. They have the structure of their argument, and the case will go up to a higher court. In the meantime, the police apparently stopped her on the way home. They were obviously looking for something. Finally, they told her that her rear view mirror wasn't legal."

Father laughed, his mouth turned down. "It's not hard to imagine what the police are doing to the Negro man, Mr. Brown, who had the gall to put his name on the suit."

"But what did Helene say in the testimony?" asked Mother. Forgetting my father's briskness, she leaned excitedly toward the conversation. "I know she even went to Mrs. Johnson's house to talk to her children and their friends. How I wish I could be helpful like that!"

"She said that, as a social worker, she could testify to the negative psychological effects on a Negro child of having to attend a segregated school. You know, the School Board had defended itself by saying that the Brown girl's school was as good as the white school. Helene was careful not to be disrespectful of the work of the Negro teachers. But she insisted that it didn't matter what the school's quality was, since segregation itself implied by definition that the Negro was inferior." Micha shrugged. "It's obviously long overdue, this integration, though Mordecai makes some interesting arguments about why Negroes should be wary, given the daily prejudice they'll face from whites. They will also lose the dignity of their autonomous culture."

"Against integration?" Mother was indignant.

"Mordecai isn't against integration," Father reassured her, his voice now softer—and I was also pleased to see him willing to explain Mordecai's side. "But he points out, for example, that Negro principals and teachers may lose their jobs to whites, who won't care about transmitting their culture or educating their—"

"Lureen Johnson already lost her job," I interrupted.

"*Quatsch*! Ridiculous!" Mother cut in with an angry toss of her head. "Everybody is the same inside."

Father shrugged irritatedly. "And everybody wants a white Protestant culture?"

"Oh, we never had such problems in Germany," cried Anna Mandelbaum.

"We didn't?" Mother snapped. "Maybe, because we were the Negroes."

"Well, it was quite different than it is for Negroes. Better and then worse, at least in Hungary," Micha laughed roughly. "For one thing, until Hitler, a Jew could disappear into the gentile culture. A Negro can't."

Mother touched her strong cheekbones. Sometimes she said she wished we all looked more Jewish. And Father was ashamed that he had been able to fool the Nazis and pass through their line.

"Still, we should have gone to Israel," wailed Mrs. Mandelbaum. "I tell Hans each day: we should have gone to Israel!"

"It would be a hard life there too," Mother said wistfully, her hand still on her cheek.

"We have no business in Palestine." Micha was annoyed. "It will only cause trouble, Jews pushing their way into the middle of the Arabs."

Father had stepped away from Mother. Now he tilted his head from side to side, as if jiggling loose a worthwhile contribution. "You can't call it Jewish land after two thousand years. Anyway, I agree," he said slowly, "it would have been better if they had given the Jews part of Australia. There they wouldn't have had to displace anyone."

"We are the Jews of the diaspora. We have to learn to live in America," said Hans. Sugar from *butterkuchen* lined his lips. "We have to be grateful for America."

Anna Mandelbaum was sniffing pathetically. "In Europe we didn't have polio." She pulled a lace handkerchief from her dress pocket and wiped the red rims of her eyes.

"Of course we did!" insisted Mother.

"No, we didn't," Micha said with authority.

"See? See what I said," Hans shook his head. "The flooding makes everyone a little crazy. We should play music, where we are simply obedient to the score."

Father drank to the end of his coffee cup and turned toward the piano. As he stood searching through the music, he called to me sternly. "Eva, better get out your violin and begin tuning."

*F*or nearly two weeks, the Kaw had receded and risen slightly, promising and taunting, but usually reassuring everyone that it was on its way down. In some neighborhoods like Seaman across the river, people had twice left their homes on the spur of the moment, returning each time with renewed hope to dry out their rugs and furniture and start again. As the older people on the block were saying that summer, none of the previous floods had been nearly so bad. And then one afternoon it rained in hard sheets, with a wind that splashed the rain against the window panes and shattered the casements. Several tree branches came thumping down along Lindenwood and lay like fallen antlers across lawns and blocked the sidewalk. In the air was a cool unsettled smell, like that of an animal on the prowl. I had been sitting with Mrs. Rogers on her front porch swing when a strong wind turned unexpectedly and showered us with a sudden blast. The maple tree by the side of her porch creaked and groaned, and an instant later a huge branch ripped away and lay broken and dangling.

"See what they mean about this one being the worst?" Mrs. Rogers stood and wrung the water from her blouse.

I had jumped back from the sound of the cracking branch, but my clothes were soaked.

"I'm going to have to get someone to cut off that limb before it falls onto the porch." She gathered her cigarettes to go inside, and I made a dash across the street.

Mother stood in her sleeveless housedress before the kitchen sink, vigorously scrubbing old pots. Sarah was pulling out even more pots from the wooden cabinet beneath the counter.

"You'd better change before you catch cold." Mother glanced up at me.

"Don't worry." I held out my arms that had become covered with goosebumps.

In the bathroom where I hung my wet clothes, the bathtub was full of tepid water, as though someone had taken a bath and forgotten to pull out the plug. I started to let the stale water drain, but something stopped me. Back in the kitchen, I watched Mother and Sarah work with mysterious concentration on the pots and pans.

"Why are you doing this?"

Mother turned her worried face toward me. "On the radio they say the Kaw is close to breaking through the sandbag dike near the waterworks. If it does, we won't have any more healthy water."

"Mrs. Rogers said it's getting to be worse than the flood of 1925," I announced. "She was just a little girl then, but she can remember and her Father used to talk about it."

Mother had turned back to her pots, too preoccupied for my historical information.

"She says her father would be livid if he were alive." I was repeating the very word Mrs. Rogers had used. "She says he would really be *livid*, because he warned everybody they should get the army to put in the dam." The word dam seemed wrong to me; I tried to recall whether she had said dike or dam, and what the difference might be.

"Mr. Rogers doesn't know everything," said Sarah.

"Her father's name couldn't have been Mr. Rogers," I reminded Sarah. "I don't know what his name was."

I went down to the basement to look for more utensils. In a corner that smelled of mildew, dank soil, and lint from the washing machine, I found an old pail and the pressure cooker Mother used for late summer canning. It occurred to me that, since Mrs. Rogers had been sitting out with me, she probably didn't know she ought to save water. Upstairs, I set the pots by the telephone and dialed her number. My heart was thumping from excitement, I rarely made calls.

"Hello, Mrs. Rogers. This is Eva from across the street. Mother says everybody should save water, because the waterworks may get flooded."

Her voice seemed small and uncertain at the other end of the line, but she knew what I meant. "Thank you, honey," she said. "And you tell your mother thanks."

I picked up my heavy vessels and carried them to the kitchen table. I was feeling good, elated even, to be so useful a part of this important event.

"Who did you just telephone?" asked Mother.

"Mrs. Rogers. I told her about the water."

"That's nice," she nodded approvingly. "How is her husband?"

"He wrote her his own letter the other day."

"Oh, good. At least that's solved," said Mother, but she sounded preoccupied.

A few minutes later, scrubbing out a pot, I mused, "Water water everywhere and not a drop to drink."

The tense lines in Mother's forehead drew outward and disappeared in her thick hair as she began to laugh. Through her laughing eyes, she was looking at me with rare and open affection.

I laughed too, even happier than before.

"Water water everywhere and not a drop to drink," Sarah sang out, slapping her thighs, and letting out a raucous giggle.

Father came home from work early. He was amusing himself by singing the passionate Hugo Wolf *lieder* to his own piano accompaniment when the telephone rang. He seemed uncertain as he held the phone from his ear, his hand over the receiver. "I'm being asked to be a responsible citizen again," he smiled ironically. "It's Mr. Cotter."

Mother wiped a stray wisp of hair from her forehead. "*Ach!* Again? What a tragedy if they can't save the waterworks!"

"What shall I say?" Father looked impatient.

"What about your cold?" Mother worried. "You're finally getting better. Maybe I should go for you. Can't women go?"

Father thought a moment, ignoring her question. "Yah, I'll come." Hanging up, he grinned to himself, pleased to have been asked back.

"I hope it's not dangerous," Mother fretted.

"No more than before."

"You'd better go up and rest, if you're going to be out in the rain all night." Her forehead was suddenly tense and drawn. "I'll make the children be very quiet."

"In a while," Father said, returning to the piano and beginning to sing the dramatic *lieder* with his half-monotone voice.

Sarah had been standing by the telephone, and now she started to cry.

"What's wrong?" asked Mother, ready to spring to her aid.

Tears fell over her chubby cheeks and she stood helplessly by the telephone.

"What's wrong?" Mother ran to her side and knelt to hug her.

"I don't want Daddy swept away in the storm," Sarah sobbed, sticking her thumb in her mouth.

"Oh, he won't get hurt. He's a big man."

"Yes, he will! He'll catch a cold and get swept away by the river." Her face looked streaked and gooey.

"David, come talk to your daughter," Mother pleaded.

Father turned from the piano bench, but continued playing softly. "She's just repeating your silly fears. Anyway, I'll be all right. I won't go anywhere dangerous." He gave Sarah a gentle amused smile.

"Look," Mother pointed to the window. "The wind is lessening and the rain is even slowing down."

We all looked out at the drops which fell vertically, leaving the window panes untouched for the first time that afternoon.

When Father went upstairs to nap, Sarah and I sat on the floor in front of the radio to listen to the news. The announcer's voice was brisk and harsh, like a chopping machine for carving out stories. A lumberyard near the river had caught fire, said the announcer, and logs were floating aflame down the Kaw. Streets had turned into gushing rivers, with birds, clocks and furniture hurtling along. One house had even been swept up and sent downstream as if it were a small boat. Mayor Wilke was ordering everyone in North Topeka to evacuate. I had never heard the Mayor speak before, but now the announcer introduced him and here he was in person, offering his authority on the radio. There would be twenty thousand people who needed homes, said the Mayor. Many churches were opening their doors to the evacuees, and he was also asking the civic center—where Sarah and I had watched the Barnum & Bailey three-ringed Circus—to clear its scheduled events to allow for living quarters. I imagined people staking little living room plots in the arenas where the clowns and lions had danced.

"I have to call Mrs. Johnson," said Mother, who had been pacing. Stopping abruptly, she went over to the telephone. I could hear above the radio that she was letting the number ring many times. "I wonder if the telephone line is down," she worried. "It sounds funny."

"Want me to listen?" I asked, getting up. I took the phone from her and listened: it didn't sound like anything I had heard before.

"Anyway, the Mayor says the water is still okay," I reassured her, with one ear again to the radio. "He said the flood hasn't gotten into the purifying tanks."

"What?" She had put down the phone and was standing distractedly.

"Does that mean we can pour out our pots of water?"

"The pots? No! Not yet!"

The announcer was talking about flooding in Manhattan and Kansas City. Suddenly Mother came over and snapped off the radio.

"Efa, why don't you read Sarah a story?"

"Mummy!" whined Sarah, who looked about to cry again. "I don't want everything to float away down the river."

Mother shook her head. "It won't. We live in a nice dry house on a little bit of hill," she said, as if reciting a nursery rhyme. "We're very safe."

"Actually, it's getting interesting now," I bravely told Sarah. "Soon we're going to be in history books, and everyone will read about us. Isn't that right, Mother?"

"I don't know."

"We will," I said, feeling the importance that swept through the air on the rain. "We will!"

"Well maybe," Mother looked doubtful.

$\mathcal{B}$ eyond the music rack, water glazed the studio window and curled and peeled away. I was trying the fingering Miss Rideaux had just worked out for me on a new Bartok exercise. While she stood beside me in her lumpy brown dress, as isolated and sturdy as a lone tree trunk, I could sense her stocky fingers pantomiming the notes in mid air. Although the music was odd and discordant, it wasn't as difficult as I had feared, and my hand slipped forward easily to the higher notes that had to be taken in second and third positions. Across Kansas Avenue, the buildings seemed to melt and bend like candles in the heat and then straighten up as their sharp outlines re-emerged. For an instant I thought I saw Mother and Sarah come out of a store, but when I again lifted my eyes from the notes the woman and child had disappeared.

"I think you've got it," said Miss Rideaux. "You just need to practice so that you can pay attention to the timing."

Gratefully, I lowered my violin and stole a glance at the little clock on her piano. It was nearly time to leave.

"Do I get a star for Palestrina?" I asked politely.

"Hmn. Not a gold one, but red if you wish." Miss Rideaux shuffled through a wooden drawer for the tiny tinseled stickers she pasted above my completed pieces in a strictly graded system of rewards. Her curly hair, which had once been a light blond, was drying out and blanching twig-like with age. Around her, the smell of the room was musty and sad in the damp morning. I turned to pack up my violin, glancing out the runny window as I loosened the hairs of my bow.

"Oh look!" I cried. Below in the street a lone horse raced along the avenue.

Miss Rideaux came to the window just as the horse disappeared into the rain.

"Did you see it?" I asked.

"No, what?"

"It was a horse, without a rider."

"Really?" She stood, wide pale arms crossed, beside me at the window.

I returned to close my violin case and put on my yellow slicker.

"It was good of you to come out in this weather, dear, especially with all the flooding," Miss Rideaux said as she held open the door. "It means you take your violin seriously."

"Mother brought me downtown." I thought of telling her that Mother had considered cancelling my lesson, since Father had still been out on the dikes when it was time to go. But I was too anxious to leave to prolong the conversation.

"Well, see you next week, same time. And don't forget to count. You tend to want to rush ahead."

"Okay." I leaned toward the narrow hall, ready to bound down the dark stairway.

"Your father doesn't have a metronome, does he?"

"I don't think so." I glanced up at Miss Rideaux's forlorn broad face. She never wanted me to leave and searched for ways to detain me once the lesson was over. "Okay, bye. Mom's probably waiting."

"You tell her thanks for bringing you."

"Okay."

"Bye, dear."

I raced down the stairs, my violin case clattering against the railing. I was hoping for another sight of the horse.

"Be careful of your violin, dear!" Miss Rideaux called down.

The bottom of the darkened stairs ended in a tiny musty hallway extending to the dirty glass front door. I had expected Mother and Sarah to be waiting. What could have caused their delay? First Father was out all night and who knew when he would come home; and now Mother, who was always exactly on time where she promised, was missing. I gazed the length of Kansas Avenue: because of the flood, few cars were out, and the wet street, with water rushing along the gutters, looked desolate and wide. Suddenly I heard the sounds of horses' feet against the pavement, and a wild brown horse with a heavy black mane flew into view. As it passed, moving away from the river, the horse's fiery eyes searched out the street. Just beyond my door, it came to a stop, shook its head violently, and raced on. I pressed my face to the wet glass and watched it disappear. Then I went outside and stood under the eaves of the building to get still another glimpse of the runaway animal.

"Here we are! Sorry we're late," Mother said in her forced cheery voice that always made me suspicious.

"Did you see the horse?" I asked, wondering if that was what was wrong.

"Certainly."

"We saw three already," said Sarah.

Mother's arms were filled with packages she had bought during my class hour. "Did Miss Rideaux think we were wrong to come out in all this for a music lesson?" she asked guiltily.

"Mother, she's a music teacher!"

"At least she was able to earn her money. Which she needs," Mother laughed. "How was your lesson?"

"Okay. Is Father home yet?"

"Yes, we just called. He and Mr. Cotter came home tired but fine."

"He said the National Guard overslept this morning," Sarah nodded confidently.

"What did you buy?"

"Emergency things, in case the flood keeps us at home."

"Look, here comes another," Sarah pointed. "No, more!"

Two speckled gray horses were galloping through the rain. Mother, Sarah and I moved out toward the curb. A car honked, another slowed down at the side of the avenue. A minute later, half a dozen horses were running past us. The street looked like an eerie race track in which none of the horses had riders.

An old man with a white mustache leaned against his cane. "They're from the packing company," he said to himself and the gathering crowd.

"Hey, gideyup!" some boys called out.

"The packing plant flooded early this morning," said the old man. "They tried to get all the horses out in vans, but a lot escaped."

"I thought they made pork down there," someone said.

"Pigs—they kept all them together. But not the horses."

"The state hospital flooded this morning," Mother said to no one in particular, and the foreign sound of her words seemed to tumble sadly on the rainy cement. "They don't have water, but the patients are safe."

"At least the men seem to be saving the waterworks," a woman turned to us.

"Yes, my husband was out there all night." Mother looked up proudly.

Two golden horses raced by, neck and neck. They were beautiful and strong and never should be eaten!

"Running for their dear lives," quipped a young man in a cowboy hat.

"I suspect there'll be a truck coming up the avenue to git 'em," said his friend.

"Whoopee!" The man slapped his hat against his leg.

Suddenly I felt as if my breakfast were inching its way up my throat.

"Here comes another," said the friend. It was a horse the color of glowing copper.

"Hey! I'm gonna mount him," said the cowboy, putting his hat back on and pretending to dash into the street.

"Are you all right? You look a little green," said Mother, shifting her packages.

"Those horses were going to die, weren't they?" I asked. I swallowed hard and my violin hung heavy in my hand.

"Yah," she said.

"Dog food," Sarah rolled her eyes.

"Also, some people eat horse meat," Mother explained brightly, but her face looked as though she needed taking care of.

As I felt for her hand, I pictured the gorgeous wild horses escaping their deaths by bravely swimming the turbulent waters. Then they had run along Kansas Avenue in search of safety; they'd come half a mile before reaching where we stood. I couldn't bear the thought of them being killed. The horses had struck out on their own, not knowing when or where they'd find a place to hide. They should be rewarded for fighting against their fate.

"I wish I could help hide them from the meat packing men," I said softly to Mother.

A white horse with a long thick mane galloped by, looking confused and insecure. Its hide gleamed and stretched over the taut muscles of its thighs. Wanting to help guide its escape, I gazed the length of Kansas Avenue. At the north end, the street sloped downward to the dirty swollen river, where the meat packing company was now under rolling water. Looking south, the stores thinned out into a few low lying buildings, and eventually, far beyond my view, opened out into farmland, wet and muddy, on all sides.

II
THE REFUGEES

*F*inally it was a glorious blue sunny day! A beautiful day! For the first time in weeks—was it months?—the sky spread overhead in an endless cavern of cornflowers. Even the warm air smelled sweet and fresh. I opened the windows of my pink lace room and happily let the breeze sweep over me. From behind the garage by the alley came the sugary scent of honeysuckle vines. Just as I had always suspected, the danger and trouble were only temporary, and now everything would return to normal. With the sun shining its brilliant hot July yellow, the water would soon dry up all around town. The waterworks had been saved. We had emptied nearly all our pans of water, and Mother was her normal self again. Mrs. Johnson had even called us: she was staying outside Topeka with her sister-in-law, Lureen; but soon her house would emerge from under water, I felt sure, and she and her family would be able to go home.

I sprinkled a little extra food over the water of my fish bowl to give my goldfish a celebration treat. They came swimming to the surface and sucked with their orange toothless mouths. The flood had come and gone. I felt as if I had won a mysterious contest or gotten something free of charge—as though I'd been through a war without having to run for my life. Yet it was true: we were all safe, my pink lace room was dry and neat.

And now I could begin to plan for the rest of summer. I would have to use each day carefully, there weren't that many left. In less than a month, two weeks before school began, I would have my birthday. The thought made my stomach tighten with new possibilities of disaster. But I would make it work out right this year, tell everyone exactly what I wanted. The way the flood had vanished made me confident. I would order a chocolate cake with gleaming chocolate icing. Mother would give me patent leather shoes for special occasions. I imagined a party in the backyard on a sunny afternoon with the trees swaying in the breeze. A table with a pink tablecloth and pink napkins would be set in the middle of the lawn. The trouble was, I didn't have any friends my own age to invite. Not Marilyn Sue, or anyone else. But even that didn't necessarily matter. . .

I could hear the creaking of Mother's chair in her bedroom. From my door, I saw her sitting by her window, sewing.

"What are you doing?" I asked, going in and plunking myself down at the edge of her bed.

"Putting identification marks on our bedding to lend to the refugees."

"Ma, the people are called evacuees," I corrected, wanting to prevent her from imagining that she and they were the same.

Mother shrugged. "I'm going to take these sheets and towels to the Presbyterian church." She bit off the end of a thread and stuck her needle in the spool. "If you like, you may come along."

I leaned against the bed; suddenly I felt stingy and mean. "Is everyone doing this?"

Mother didn't look up. "I can't answer for everyone."

"But why is it your business?"

"Efa."

"I'm just asking."

"Are you coming?" she asked, beginning to sort her linens into piles.

I didn't really want to see the people who had suffered from the flood: I could tell that they would only make me feel the problem wasn't entirely over. But looking at the inside of a new church interested me. "I hope we're going to take the car," I said, knowing the answer. "No one but us ever walks—I don't see why we even have a car."

"Efa, cut it out."

We stopped in front of the Rogers' and Mother left me on the sidewalk while she went to tell Sarah where we were going. I could see Sarah and Bobby behind the shade of the front window, and then Mother stood inside the screen door, chatting with Mrs. Rogers, who had a scarf tied around her head. I looked up at the giant oaks that arched in a great green lace of leaves over our street. Deep blue filled the spaces high beyond the leaves. Even the birds were rejoicing in the perfect day. Was it one bird or two having a conversation? I could only see the green filigree and the marvelous blue sky.

"*Gott*! That poor woman is worrying about her husband." Mother came out shaking her head but laughing merrily and carrying a victorious bundle of several folded sheets. "Look! I got her to contribute. I think it even lifted her spirits."

I helped stuff the new sheets into the bags. We had four heavy bags, two for each to carry.

"It's nice and hot today. Summer at last!" Mother squinted happily at the sky.

I gazed upward with her. Something flitted from branch to leaf. Where had all the squirrels been during the rain?

At the end of the block, the old woman with hair like bluish cotton candy sat on her porch swing. Seeing us, she waved with a handkerchief.

"Should we ask her if she wants to give linens?" Mother asked with conspiratorial excitement.

"Ma, let's go now."

"I bet she has drawers of sheets she hasn't used in years!"

"Ma! My bags are already too heavy," I said, wanting to rein her in.

"You're right, we have enough," Mother agreed, and gave the woman a friendly, chastened wave.

We walked briskly down several streets of wooden houses with boxy front porches and flat, soggy treeless yards. Here and there new one-story houses sat like marshmallows on barren lots. Tiny trees had been planted and leaned precariously against supporting poles, but it would be years before they gave canopies of shade. High in the blue sky, a long feathery cloud rested like the vertebrae of a lazy crocodile.

"Look," I pointed upward with my nose.

"*Hübsch*, pretty," she nodded, but I could tell she was nervous to move on and deposit our load.

As we turned a corner, we faced a large brick building with a narrow steeple and white trimmed windows. "The First Presbyterian Church," read a standup billboard in Gothic black letters. The parking lot at the side of the church looked as if preparations for a rummage sale were underway: people's furniture and crates had been piled hurriedly in random tumbledown stacks. Someone had tacked a crayoned cardboard sign, CHECK IN HERE, against the side door. I stood back a moment, hesitating.

"Come, *süsse*," Mother pushed me ahead.

Even as we went gingerly down a narrow flight of stairs, the smell of dust and mildew assailed my nostrils and made me want to gag. The vast underground auditorium had been cleared of its metal chairs, which were now stacked along the edges. In little clusters throughout the enormous space stood cots with suitcases, cribs, and buggies beside them. Some families had strung rope from a wall to a column, and laundry hung like pathetic colored flags around the little makeshift home areas. People dozed here and there, their arms flung across their faces or one leg dangling from a cot, and in a corner some children played with blue and red wooden blocks. On the stage, rimmed in burgundy velvet curtains, long tables had been set with plastic dishes for the next meal. Spaghetti sauce was being cooked somewhere in another room, but the smell came mingled with sweat and mildew. I took short shallow breaths as I trailed behind Mother's hurried steps through the maze of cots. Then, as we set down our bags, I cautiously put my hand over my nose.

"Good afternoon." A plump white-haired woman smiled at us with small pearly teeth. She looked as though she should be swinging on a clean, shady front porch like our neighbor.

"I'm Mrs. Hoffman. This is my daughter. We've come with the linens," Mother announced to the woman. Her voice sounded staccato and machine-like; suddenly I wished I hadn't come.

"That's very nice of you. We sure can use them," the woman warbled delicately.

I sat down on a folding chair at the side of the desk and focused my attention on the woman's silky church dress. Tiny lavender fans spread out on a navy background and alternated with winding flowers bound in trailing bows. A pink patterned apron protected her lap, and a string of pearls decorated her soft neck.

"We just had a couple come in with three kids," she shook her head, and her pearls slid back and forth on her silky dress. "I don't know whether they waited until the last minute, or what, but they don't have a tooth brush to their name!"

With my hand still protecting my nose, I peered cautiously over the cots in search of the newly arrived family whom the woman seemed to be criticizing.

"Sometimes you don't have time to plan when you have to run," Mother said stiffly.

"Yes, now it's a terrible thing, this flood, and it's not going to recede for a while," the woman said, but her dainty voice floated right over the trouble. She bent to write Mother's contribution on an inventory list.

"I have marked all my linen." Mother showed the neatly stitched initials on the corners. Then she gave a throaty laugh. "Unfortunately, my neighbor didn't think to lend anything until I dropped by."

I turned away and stared exasperatedly at the butterscotch tiled wall.

"Oh, we can mark them right here," the woman was saying, having missed Mother's criticism of Mrs. Rogers.

"*Eins, zwei, drei, vier*—these are all mine."

"Just fine, just fine."

"It's very important that you do this. It's very important to help people who lose everything." I glanced back at Mother: her eyes were glued to the woman, as if she had just gotten off a roller coaster and were unsure of her grounding. "Some people don't know what it's like. But it doesn't matter, whether it's a war or a flood. It could be persecution. I know. It's all the same. If people have lost everything, it's all the same, there's no difference." Mother nodded rapidly. Her words seemed to be blocked by there being so much to say, and her eyes were swimming behind her glasses.

"I suspect so." The woman looked a little nervous at Mother's outpouring.

Mother was staring out over the sea of cots filled with people talking and dozing. A woman carried a basin of wet laundry. A child cried. "You don't have any Negro families here?" she noted, and a new anxiety put a quivery sharp edge to her voice.

"Well, no. Their churches take care of their own."

"But several thousand Negroes have been hurt by the flood." Mother seemed uncertain about how to proceed, and I worried that she might try to take back the linens.

"Well, I suspect so." The woman sat down and began to check her inventory.

"And most of the Negro churches are near the river, in the flooded areas, aren't they?" continued Mother, holding her handbag forlornly at her side.

"I suppose. 'Course the Civic Center took in over ten thousand."

"I should probably check if anyone else needs a home. In an emergency is it right not to take someone in?"

"Come on, Mummy, let's go." I took her free hand, embarrassed for the excess of criticism and concern she was showing.

The woman glanced up with a quick pearly smile, and her nostrils were delicate and fine. "Well, thanks again for your real nice help."

"Maybe you need other things, clothing—"

"We're okay right now." The woman was impatiently twirling her narrow black pen.

"One collects so quickly." Mother looked pointedly at her. "Twelve years ago I had nothing."

"Mummy, I want to see the church." I gave her a tug.

Mother shook herself as if out of sleep. "Oh, excuse me, one last thing. Can I show my daughter your church?"

"Surely, help yourself," the woman nodded. "That door over there leads right up into the vestry. You're also welcome to attend on Sundays," she added. "We have services at nine-thirty and again at eleven."

"Thank you very much," Mother said tensely.

I pulled at her arm to stop her from saying more, and she followed me obediently as we threaded our way among the cots. In the children's corner, a thin woman with a long bony face was changing a little boy's corduroys while he ran his red truck over the floor.

"You and Sarah have to look through your toys. I'm sure you have books and puzzles you no longer play with," said Mother.

"Ma! We just gave a lot," I cautioned.

The stairs to the vestry were narrow and carpeted in burgundy red. Gingerly, I pushed open a heavy wooden door at the top. We were in a small room lined with white robes like the ones Reverend Thomas had wanted to buy his choir for summer. I tiptoed carefully past the choir robes, then walked through an open door which led into the main body of the church. The large high nave was all white wood, bright and clean, with red carpeting on the floor and red velvet cushioned pews. Colored light filtered in from the stained glass windows and turned the white walls into a kaleidoscope. The altar was white and gold in a filigree design, and a giant gold cross leaned over it from high above. Everything was clean and pure. A soft fragrance filled the air.

"Isn't it beautiful?" I whispered. This is why I had come, and it was all worthwhile! There was nothing of the basement up here. I felt the smooth red velvet of the cushions with my finger tips and sat gingerly at the edge of a pew.

Mother twisted her mouth and looked suspiciously about her. She seemed worn out and uneasy, as she sat down next to me.

"Wouldn't you like to go to a church like this?" I begged.

"It doesn't look very religious to me." Suddenly tears were glistening on Mother's cheeks. Afraid to look at her red-rimmed eyes, I fidgeted with the prayer books. "I believe more in what they're doing downstairs," she said determinedly.

I pictured again the smelly room filled with displaced people. It seemed so desperate, while this was peaceful, clean and still. "Ma, but they don't have any Negroes," I reminded her.

Mother shivered.

"Do you think Reverend Oliver Brown's church is flooded?" I asked, suddenly worried.

"Reverend Brown?"

"Ma, the man who wants his daughter to come to school with everyone else."

"Perhaps. If he lives near Mrs. Johnson."

"Lureen Johnson's house is safe, and she teaches school."

"Yes, but there's more than one Negro neighborhood, dearie."

"How come Reverend Oliver Brown wants to integrate and Reverend Thomas doesn't?" I continued, though I hated to bring my confused thoughts into the silence of the church.

"The minister of this church is obviously not very interested in integration either," Mother shook her head.

"Anyway, I think it's beautiful here," I insisted, quietly running my fingers along my cushion. "I wish I could go to a church like this."

Mother sighed. "I should take you to a synagogue. Do you understand what it means for someone not to know they're Jewish?" She wiped her eyes with her forefinger.

I didn't answer, though I was suddenly on guard and my heart had begun pounding.

"I'll tell you a story," she said in a low quivery voice. She laid her hand on my arm to pull me closer, but I resisted and sat stiffly beside her. "It comes from the time when your Father and I left Vienna. Maybe I already told you about the transport train of children that was allowed to escape. It was December, 1938."

I nodded, not wanting to hear more than the vague details I already knew, and gazed around the sparkling white room. What if someone came in?

"There were children of every background. Children who had never been to a synagogue and didn't believe in God but who had been given a strong Zionist education and knew Yiddish or Hebrew. Children who were only half or a quarter Jewish and hadn't even known until the very night they were brought down to the train. Also Orthodox Jews, who had Kosher food packed in their knapsacks and wore long ringlets at their ears, *pais*— you've never seen them." She shook her head regretfully. But then a disapproving thought seemed to cross her mind, and her face grew pained. "I don't know, there were some who said that those Eastern Jews with their queer habits, who made such a show of being Jewish, also irritated the Nazis and so made it harder on the rest. You know, when you live in a country, you have to try to fit in."

I was listening with half an ear, but my eye was on the door to the room where the choir robes hung. Was it right to talk about us Jews in a church?

"All these children were being sent out to be saved." Mother shivered next to me. "Some were going to Palestine—those were the Youth Aluyah groups, and I had hoped to go there too. But your father wanted to try for England. Anyway, without Hitler, the children in our transport would have had nothing in common, they would have never met, but now they were all together. Their lives were suddenly joined. And your father and I, we were the counselors. We took care that they ate the food their parents had packed, and washed their hands, and took a nap.

"The train drove through Austria and then Germany during the night. How we held our breaths for fear the Nazis would change their minds and turn us back! But everybody on the train had been given permission to leave, and they let us go free. The next morning we were in Holland, and your father and I had to help the children climb down from the train with their little packs and change to a boat to cross the English channel. These children didn't know where they were going or what would happen to them. Your father and I hardly knew for ourselves. Many of them never saw their parents again."

The room was utterly quiet. Not even the sounds from downstairs penetrated. We had been left completely alone. Mother's warm hand still lay heavily on my arm and her cheeks were wet with tears, but she let them glisten and her face was relaxed with deep sorrow.

Softly, she began again. "In the refugee camp, in England, some of the children cried at night, a few got angry or mean or refused to eat. The ones who had been given a religious or Zionist training, or who knew they were Jewish by other means, they were all right. I don't mean they didn't suffer. But they had some understanding of why they had to leave Austria and come to this strange place. They were prepared. But for those children who hadn't even known they were Jewish, or who knew but thought it didn't count, life was terrible! *Schrecklich*! I remember one boy, maybe your age, he began to wet his bed. Imagine! And another was so angry, he was always fighting." She stroked my arm. "That's why, dearie, I always want you to know you are Jewish."

Inside a photograph album, I had seen a picture of Mother and Father standing with a dozen children by a wrought iron gate. The boys had short pants on and the girls wore awkward dresses. I knew the photograph had been taken at the entrance to the refugee camp in England, where they had settled. But it didn't look much different than any yellowing picture of teachers and students from a small school. Nothing in the orphaned children's squinting smiles or Mother's and Father's hair-blown faces showed that something terrible had happened. Mother's story made me feel dizzy and weak in the knees.

Mother stood and let go of my arm. She was blowing her nose.

I turned to watch the colored light from the church windows dance against the white walls. "Anyway, I know I'm Jewish," I said, as if this would be sufficient to reclaim that difficult mix of being right and safe. "I really don't get confused about who I am."

"*I*t's completely unfair," I announced, and kicked the stone ledge with my saddle shoe. More and more, as the long hot days wore into August that year, my world pressed up against me, making it impossible to be generous and in good spirits. On this Saturday, water lay in a listless shallow lake on the low side of the ledge on which I was sitting, and grew deeper as the parkland dropped toward the creek. My optimism had come with the sun, but I had been wrong: the effects of the flood were clinging everywhere, and in new ways—especially in our house!

"What is?" Sarah asked timidly.

"You know what." I didn't feel like explaining. I wasn't mad at Sarah, but she was part of the problem. "Because Daddy really could stop Mother, if he wanted."

"You could have my room." Sarah raised her small dark eyebrows with an effort to please.

"And where are you going to stay?" I snapped. Over by the bandstand, the bridge was completely under water. In normal times you could see that someone had written I SUCK DICK in large letters under the cement arch of the bridge. Though I had seen the older children snicker, I couldn't figure out who Dick was. "Mother is an Indian-giver," I said.

"Maybe the family from the flood will be nice," Sarah offered fearfully.

"I don't care whether they're nice or not, they're not sleeping in my pink room!" I hated the dirty water that continued to flood every low area of town. Although we'd been warned of pollution, a boy jumped from the roof of the band shelter, as if it were a diving board, into the lake that now covered where people once sat to hear concerts. Children were also swimming on the tennis courts at the other end of the park, and I thought I saw Marilyn Sue jumping among them. "Anyway, they're a dumb farm family," I added with a certain fierce gratification at this safe area of bigotry. "I don't see why they can't stay in their church until their house is okay."

"Mummy said some of their house floated away." Sarah looked nervous.

"Most of it's still there."

"Maybe they'll repair it fast!" She raised her brows hopefully, trying to encourage me with positive thoughts.

"Fast! Do you know how long it takes to repair a house that's all wrecked? They could be living with us when you're as old as I am."

Sarah sucked her thumb and stared at the water. I thought of telling her to take it out, but I didn't even have the strength to order her around.

"Mrs. Rogers has a spare bedroom, and she's not taking anyone in from the flood," I pointed out. "Why does it have to be us? Why does it always have to be us?"

Tears suddenly trickled down Sarah's chubby cheeks and over the thumb that plugged her mouth.

"What's wrong?"

Sarah rocked back and forth on the cement wall and the tears now streamed freely, glazing her face and hand.

"What's wrong?" I asked again, this time more gently.

"I don't know why you don't want to sleep with me," she gasped, smudging her runny cheeks.

"It's not that," I lied.

"You could put your bed back where it was before."

"And what about Grandmother?" I asked. "You think she wants strangers in her room? That was *her* room, you know. In a way, it still is. I'm just staying there because she can't be there anymore."

Sarah stood up on the wall and looked at me red-eyed.

"Anyway, you should be furious too. You're losing your room, too."

"I don't know."

"I'm telling you, you should be as mad as I am. What's wrong is wrong."

Sarah started walking along the wall.

"But if I tell Mother she was wrong to give my room away, will you agree with me?" I demanded, standing up. "Where are you going?"

"I want to go swimming," she said, slowing down to wait for me.

"But you agree we should stick together? We really have to do something to stop her." Bits of grass and debris floated on the muddy water.

Sarah nodded. "Let's go over there."

The flood water did look more appetizing by the courts. Glimpses of blue appeared in the brownish water that hid the nets and allowed only the tops of the poles to peek through. I looked to see if Marilyn Sue was there, but, if she had been before, she was now gone.

"We have our typhoid shots, but Mother will worry about polio if we go in." I smiled at the possibility of a terrible illness putting a halt to her big plans.

At lunch, with my hair still wet from swimming, I took a section of the newspaper from Father to protect myself for the little project on which I had gotten Sarah to agree: we would talk to neither Mother nor Father until justice had been done. In fact, it was interesting reading the paper. One story reported that a woman had been electrocuted while searching through the remains of her home. Because of this tragedy, inspectors were going through the heavily damaged areas and marking the houses "approved" or "condemned." The Chamber of Commerce was also issuing identification permits to all North Topeka residents, and no one else would be let into the area.

I was pouring myself more milk when the doorbell rang and Father went to answer. Through the kitchen door I could see two men, one lean and tall in a hat, the other shorter and round with an open shirt, stand at the front door. They began to speak to Father in low voices. I would have asked Mother why he wasn't letting them in, but I had sworn not to talk.

"A doctor from Chicago is coming to Topeka to interview flood victims," she glanced over at me with victory in her eyes.

"He wrote a book on World War II D.P.'s and wants to compare the effects of a natural and a human-made disaster. You see?"

Sarah was lazily kicking the side of her chair as she picked peanut butter and jelly out of her brown bread.

I heard Father say something about Helene.

"So what?" I said.

"Oops!" Sarah looked at me wide-eyed.

"So it's not just me," Mother insisted. "A doctor with a scientific background makes the same connections. All refugees are alike," she added with satisfaction.

"You were the one who said we weren't going to be in the history books," I retorted behind my newspaper.

Sarah kicked her chair and stared darkly at me.

"I guess I was wrong," Mother laughed. "Because people have been very helpful and courageous."

"He's not studying the helpful ones," I pointed out.

"The N-double-A-C-P, a subversive group?" Father's voice was suddenly raised. I saw the tall man take off his hat.

"You think he wants to study the selfish people like you," she laughed, this time with a mean tinge.

"Anyway, the man is *studying* people, not giving them other people's rooms," I said, trying not to be distracted from my side of the argument.

"You've been lucky so far." Mother put down her paper. "They should have arrived by now." She was bending her neck to watch Father and the men through the kitchen door. The conversation seemed to have gotten short-tempered, at least between Father and the short man.

Sarah continued to pick at her peanut butter, but she was staring at me and her foot beat evenly on the crossbar of the chair.

"Sarah, stop it!" I slammed down my newspaper.

"Efa, *sei ruhig*, calm down."

"I don't want them here on my birthday! And tell her to stop kicking the chair," I directed, leaping to my feet as tears threatened.

"Efa's right." Mother looked at Sarah. Then to me, "That's still a month away."

"The fifteenth. It's not so long!"

"But Eva's talking, she broke her vow," Sarah said, and began to cry as Father closed the front door and came back into the kitchen.

"What was that? Some kind of police?" Mother looked worried again.

"They were asking about Helene."

"What did you tell them?"

"That they'd be better off using government money to investigate something else."

Father looked gray, but boiling deep inside, as he sat down to finish his meal.

B ent from soggy cartons piled to his chin, a broad-faced heavy man with curly orange hair felt his way up the front porch steps. I was standing by the hedge of our shady side yard to avoid the preparations of Mother and Mrs. Johnson, who had shown up after a long absence with her plastic shopping bag of ragged work clothes. After a few minutes, the man climbed heavily back down the stairs, empty handed. At the sidewalk, he turned to wipe his ruddy freckled face with a red handkerchief and look up at our white wooden house. Then he got into his green truck, slammed the door and drove off. Although I didn't feel like talking to Mother, I went into the kitchen to find out about our new guest.

Mother wiped her hands and smiled happily. She was like someone who had been recuperating slowly from an illness and was now bursting with good health. "*Komisch*! He said his name was Rosie. Is that a man's name?"

"Rosie?"

"Yah, Rosie Williger."

The man did have pink freckled skin, and the hairs on his thick arms had been bleached golden from the sun. In coloring, Rosie Williger had looked like a tea rose; I wondered if the whole family would come in this hue.

"So, I'm afraid at last you will have to make a decision."

"I know." I jabbed my finger at a loaf of pumpernickel bread on the counter.

Mother eyed the bread quickly, then turned to gaze sharply out the window. "I had to tell Mr. Williger to leave the cartons in the hall, because I didn't know where he and his wife would stay. That's not fair. Besides, Mrs. Johnson has had to clean not knowing where to put anything."

"I thought you said his name was Rosie," I argued.

"He told me he's called Rosie, but his name is Mr. Williger. We don't even know him yet."

"Are they going to have more boxes?"

"What a question! You think a whole family has three cartons of possessions?" Mother laughed. She went to the broom closet and took out the pail and wet rag mop, keeping busy. She knew I was purposely trying to destroy her buoyant good mood.

"How can they store everything they own in a little bedroom?" I demanded.

"Some of their boxes will be stored in the basement." Mother ran the water and put the mop in the sink to clean it.

I went upstairs and stood at the door of my pink lace room. I could hear Mrs. Johnson's slow slippered footsteps next door in Sarah's room. My pajamas were on the floor, and a few books and papers were out of their shelves. My bed was unmade, the covers askew. On my own I had done what I could over the last days to destroy my nice room. Yet the mess I had created brought to mind Grandmother's last days in our house. Then the room had smelled from illness, and bathrobes, night jackets and medicine bottles were everywhere. One day while she lay quietly in bed, her gray eyes staring out large and bewildered from her already skull-like face, I had hung up her clothes. "*Danke schön,*" she had said, and had begun to hum softly a sentimental little song Mother always tried to stop her from singing. "*Du, du liegst mir in Herzen; du, du, liegst mir in Sinn,*" it went, "You lie in my heart; you lie in my thoughts."

"Ma, I need a box if I'm going to move my things!" I called out, trying to cut off the melody.

I could hear her coming to the foot of the stairs; she disliked shouting. "*Du, du liegst mir in Herzen. Weisst nicht wie gut ich dir bin.*" The complaining little song was still wailing inside my head.

"What did you say?" Mother's voice was friendly but controlled.

"I can't move my things without boxes."

"You're going to be very hot up there," Mother warned me. "You know you can't take the heat."

I glanced over my room, letting my eye dive momentarily into the magical pink land between the lace. I would rather move everything out than have Sarah and the new girl bring in their beds and clothes. Two other people in my room, Grandmother's room, would be intolerable. It would spoil everything precious I ever had. At least if I went up to the attic, Mr. and Mrs. Williger could move into the room and do whatever they wanted. I would come back untouched when it was all over. I wouldn't have to see what went on.

Mother's thick brown hair and strong tense face rose into view over the rim of the stairs.

"Is that your final decision?"

I nodded.

"We can always bring you back down with the other girls if it gets too hot, I suppose."

"I'm not sleeping with them."

"All right."

She opened the attic door and looked up toward the low rafters beyond the narrow wooden stairs. She was shaking her head as I joined her. Air as hot as from the blower of a laundry floated down from the top of the steps.

"We have to open the windows," I said meekly. In fact, I felt scared. I hated being hot, at times grew faint from the heat, and still had all of August to endure. What if the weather turned sweltering and steamy for the rest of the summer? What if we got those 100 degree afternoons when you could fry eggs on the sidewalk and the hot air got trapped in the attic room so that I could scarcely breathe?

"Why don't you go up and open the windows?" Mother said worriedly.

"You do it," I pleaded.

Mother sucked her teeth. "If you can't stand it up there long enough to open a window, you shouldn't try to live up there."

Her logic was forceful. I took a deep gulp of air and tried to hold my breath as I climbed the steep wooden steps. The stairs had never been painted and large splinters stuck out in the raw wood. At the top, the dust spun through the air and made glistening patterns in the streaked sunlight. Within an instant, my T-shirt clung to my back. I felt dizzy by the time I got to the little front window. I tried to push it up, but it wouldn't budge. The thought that I wouldn't be able to open it made me want to blank out until I was miraculously saved. From the back of my mind, I suddenly remembered the latch. Quickly, I unlocked it. Pushing the casement up, I leaned out the window and drew in the morning air that flowed sweetly and coolly over the trees. Birds chirped from hidden places, and in the crook of a branch I saw the compressed twigs of a nest.

"Remember, both windows," Mother called up.

I could sense her deciding whether or not to come up the stairs. I turned to look down the length of the attic toward the other small window at the opposite end. Pink rock wool lay like dirty cotton candy under the slant of the roof on either side, thick with the heat of the attic. An old leather suitcase stood sagging and half opened. Letters, yellowed and ragged at the edges, had tumbled out, with their foreign stamps faded and curling. A rusted box spring had been left at a kilter in the middle of the room, the wires as hot as the coils of a stove. The wind from outside cooled and dried the back of my sweaty neck, but perspiration dripped from my forehead into my eyes.

"Are you all right?" Mother called.

When I had opened the second window and come back down to the foot of the stairs, I was drenched with sweat and I could feel my cheeks inflamed from the heat.

"I'll be cooler in a minute," I apologized weakly.

Mrs. Johnson had joined us in the hall. Her high forehead below her bandanna was beaded with sweat, and her mouth was tight.

"I think it's too hot up there," Mother looked at her.

"It ain't cool nowhere today." Mrs. Johnson took her lace-rimmed kerchief from her pocket and wiped her forehead.

"You think we should move her up?"

"Is that what you want me to do next?" Mrs. Johnson looked at Mother and avoided my eyes.

For the next hour, Mrs. Johnson helped Mother and me with our trips up and down the attic stairs until most of my room, including my fish, had been transplanted onto the third floor. In

Mother's mind, she and Mrs. Johnson were partners in an exciting project; she had never looked happier and more at ease around the woman.

"I don't see why I have to move," I said to Mrs. Johnson when Mother had gone down for a moment.

"Looks like you're gonna." She leaned on her broom and looked at me from under half-closed lids. "Looks like you ain't got much choice."

"I still don't want to," I insisted, hoping to edge Mrs. Johnson into being an ally.

"The flood ain't been easy on no one," she said, and slapped her rag.

Mother returned with a little blue rug to decorate my attic room and a fan to help cool it. As she arranged the rug by the bed, she laughed merrily. "What a coincidence!" alluding to either the unused furniture she was discovering, or the return of Mrs. Johnson in time to share in the transformation of our house.

But Mrs. Johnson hung back from Mother's enthusiasm. With the passing morning, her dark face looked even more pinched and drawn.

As they stood on either side of an old trunk, ready to move it to the opposite end of the attic, Mother suddenly looked worriedly at Mrs. Johnson. "*Ach*! I should come and help you out, since you're giving us such a help."

"Psst!" Mrs. Johnson set down the heavy trunk. She fanned herself, looking around the attic, and the whites of her eyes poked fun at Mother.

"No, really, what is there to do?"

"Mud," Mrs. Johnson sighed at Mother.

"Mud?" Mother was baffled. "How do you do that?"

"Mud," Mrs. Johnson repeated. "Mud. It's just about everywhere you look. Mud. Mud! It could make you sick!"

"Well, I want to help when you're ready. Efa will come with me. Won't you, Efa?"

"You gonna get yourself all covered with mud?"

"Sure," I answered Mother, looking on uncomfortably from my displaced bed.

When my room was in order, and Mother and Mrs. Johnson had gone down, I hung my clothes on a line Mother had strung under the eaves. I imagined Mrs. Johnson's house with silt and mud suffocating every surface. Everything was thick and gray and covered with filth. There would be corn stalks outside, broken from the flood and waving awkwardly in the wind; it wasn't the kind of place anyone should have to live in. When I came downstairs, Mother was in the kitchen, mixing a Viennese torte for the Willigers.

Leaning over the counter where she worked, I demanded, "Are you really going over to Mrs. Johnson's house to help her clean off the mud?"

"*Natürlich.* Of course."

I watched her stir the ground nuts into the creamy batter. "Why didn't we take in *her* family?" I asked.

"Whose?"

"Mrs. Johnson's."

Mother beat the torte with hard vigorous strokes. "You heard," she looked at me over her glasses. "She's staying at her sister-in-law's house. Their own home just needs cleaning."

"But it's not all right now. It's covered with mud."

"They'll be able to move back in."

"I know. But they can't move back until she cleans."

"Efa! Why do you always aggravate me?" Mother asked, but she kept her eyes turned from mine.

A disturbing thought was crossing my mind. Except on those days Mrs. Johnson came to clean, we never had Negroes in our house. Helene's little talk with Mrs. Johnson had been on her cleaning day. The other people on the street, who didn't hire anyone to clean, never had Negroes in their homes. And, of course, Mrs. Rogers hadn't wanted a Negro little girl. For all Mother's wishes for a better world, she must have hung back from inviting Mrs. Johnson's family. What would Helene have done? Meanwhile, there were the Johnsons, stranded way out at Lureen's, the teacher's, house; and standing behind the Johnsons in my mind were all the Negro families Mother had worried about when we visited the Presbyterian church. As I watched Mother bend over the special cake for the Willigers, I saw her good deed turn into cowardice. I hadn't the heart to say anything further and, hanging my head with shame, went upstairs.

Mrs. Johnson was in my pink shell of a room, which was already becoming Mr. and Mrs. Williger's. The cartons Rosie had brought were stacked against one wall, where they sagged from their own soggy weight. Fresh white sheets had been wrapped over the large mattress and tightly tucked in the corners. Mrs. Johnson was down on her hands and knees scrubbing away some old stains from the floor, the delicate pink bottoms of her feet swaying rhythmically as she rubbed.

I stood for a moment, afraid to begin. Then I said quickly, "I think Mother should have let you and Mayella and your family stay here."

Mrs. Johnson looked up to give me a dark tired look.

"Really!" I said, as my heart filled with unexpected generosity and courage. "I wouldn't mind at all if *you* stayed in my room."

"You want your Mama and her friends to turn everything around all by theirselves?" Mrs. Johnson slapped her rag on the floor.

"What do you mean?"

"I mean, I'm speaking of your mama. She takes care to act kindly and she worries about these things. But I ain't gonna make trouble for her and she knows it."

Mrs. Johnson's words squeezed my heart. "Wouldn't you take *us* in if our house were flooded?" I asked.

"I s'pect." Mrs. Johnson pulled herself up from the floor and sat at the edge of the carefully made bed. She looked at me carefully, as though she were trying to figure something out. "But you folks would most likely find a better place to go."

I knew she was saying we were too elegant for her house. "But what about this?" I said, putting my hands in my pockets. "What about—would you ever adopt a white child?"

"Honey I already got four children," she sighed, and looked down at her swollen hands.

"I know. But say you didn't. Would you then?"

Mrs. Johnson pushed her cuticles with the nail of her forefinger; I could tell she was deciding whether or not to get impatient. Finally, when she had studied her fingers a moment, she said, as if impatiently reciting a lesson: "First, they wouldn't give me one. And second, if I somehow got one—let's say it was left at my door—I'd probably end up hanging from a tree by the end of the week. And third, how am I going to talk to the child's teacher if I still can't even get into a white school? Now, is that enough?" she asked, and her eyes were trying to be fierce yet they were oddly soft at their centers. "Is that enough, or do you need more reasons?"

"It's enough," I said, and turned slowly away. By the door, I stopped a moment. "Does Lureen have her job back?" I asked, though my mouth was so dry it was a near whisper.

"Yes, I s'pose she does. At least so long as Mr. Brown doesn't win his case nowhere else."

"But they might still change their mind about integration," I suggested, in a desperate new burst of courage.

"Ain't no white folks going to change their mind unless they got some law forcing them."

"Well, they might get a law," I said.

"Yeah. And by that time my kids ain't going to need an elementary school."

I looked down at my feet, which suddenly seemed to have nowhere to go. From out in the hallway, I could see Mrs. Johnson get back on her hands and knees. "I just want to make things better!" I yelled into my old room, and dug my fists into my wet eyes.

"They moved in," I said. I was sitting on the rim of the bathtub.

Father stood at the sink in a short sleeved shirt and the dark slacks he wore to the clinic. He was washing his hands in a meditative thorough way. "I know. Did you meet them?"

"Not yet." Someone had dripped toothpaste or white shoe polish on the bathmat; I nudged it with my saddle shoe.

"They came this afternoon?"

"Uh huh." I had seen them from my high window. This time there had been three: the full set. Rosie's carrot hair had gleamed in the steamy day, and his body was solid under his powerful shoulders. The mother, Mary Ellen Williger, seemed to be a stick woman. Her brown hair covered her head like a smooth cap that turned into little plastic curls at her ears, and she wore a starched dress, as if she had just walked out of a little house with a picture window, not a crowded church basement. Then there was the girl—Mother had said her name was Jolie. Even from the attic, she looked husky and big like her father. She had loped up and down the stairs, two at a time, between the truck and the front porch, her freckled arms flailing wildly. She had on a checked sundress and her thick flame pigtails bounced behind her. Sarah had appeared at the head of the steps, and they had begun to jump the stairs together, seeing who could take the most at a leap. Sarah had immediately forgotten her promise to stay away from the Willigers and was already falling into being buddies with Jolie.

Father ran his hand over his loose jowl and peered into the mirror. "I could shave," he said.

Father only shaved a second time in the evening before a concert or a holiday party at Menninger's. "You don't have to shave," I said, annoyed that he considered this a special occasion.

He took off his glasses and nodded at himself in the mirror. "I think I'll do it anyway," he sighed.

Suddenly I realized he was dawdling, looking for things to do to avoid going downstairs. "They sure are a weird family," I commented, to make conversation.

"I thought you hadn't met them." He was stirring his shaving brush in the soap to whip up lather.

"I mean looking. I watched them move in. You should have seen how excited Mother was."

Father smiled. "You don't like our house becoming an ark? Mr. Williger seems interesting. Your mother says that, besides running their little farm, he works for the railroad."

I got up from the bathtub and stood by the sink to watch Father lather his face. "You mean, he drives a train engine?" Without glasses, Father's face looked almost naked and a little embarrassing.

"I'm not sure." He glanced down at me.

"What are you going to talk to him about?"

Father laughed, and his teeth seemed yellow next to his white soap beard. "Your mother appears to be chatting quite easily with all of them."

"Yes, but that's Mommy. Anyway, I won't be able to like the girl."

Father peered in the mirror as he scraped the soap from his face. "Give her a chance. She will be interesting. You've never known anyone like her before."

"What do you mean?"

"The daughter of a railway worker. Apparently at one time they had a larger farm that was self-sustaining. They're real Kansans. Good people."

I could tell Father was preparing for the Willigers by turning them into harmless storybook creatures. "I know kids like that in school," I replied. It would be nice if I could shrink the Willigers into toy figures small enough to set on a table, but I could tell they were going to be regular size and much too real.

"Did you practice yet?" Father glanced at me over his razor.

"Daddy!"

"You're not going to stop playing the violin because the Willigers are living here, I should hope."

I looked down at the sink, where little black hair dots floated on the backs of soap globules towards the drain. "I know. But I'm not practicing the first night they're here."

"Why not? You don't think the Willigers like music?"

"I'm just not doing it."

I walked out of the bathroom and stood at the closed door to my old room. Sarah's open room was now filled with two beds that had already been used as trampolines. Sarah's books and puzzles had not been put away, or else she and Jolie had already pulled them out. Jolie's clothes spilled like colored rags from cartons at the foot of her bed. Soon—I could just see it!—mashed cookies and spilled grape juice would stain the wooden floor.

Downstairs everything was quiet. I heard voices out in the backyard: the excited talking and laughing wove together. Mother had expanded our dining room table with an extra leaf and covered it with a flowered cloth that must have been Mrs. Williger's. I stared at the pale yellow chrysanthemums spreading out under our bright fiesta plates. On any other day Mother would laugh at the tasteless effect, but tonight she had given up her own ideas to please our guests.

The sudden noise of everyone returning pinned me to my place next to the table. The air seemed to swirl and rattle. Then Rosie Williger was in the room, still larger than I had imagined from the high window, smelling of heat, and holding the freckled hand of his red-haired daughter. A vast bright plaid shirt covered his torso and arms, leaving bare a few inches of curling reddish hair at his chest and wrists. He had a freckled face, burned pink from the sun, and deep white wrinkles spread out from his bleached lashes. Jolie was skipping and twirling as she twisted up against her father. The girl had a little round nose under pale eyes. She might have been cute if she hadn't looked so sassy. Behind them stood Mrs. Williger, who could have been a sister to Mrs. Rogers, with her pointed sharp features, until she turned sideways and suddenly she was flat as a penny. She was wearing a dress of tiny print flowers on white, and from where she stood her lily of the valley perfume filled the air.

"Sit, sit, everybody. Make yourself at home!" Mother called gaily. She came through the kitchen door with a platter of pot roast and braised potatoes.

"Oh, my, look at that," said Mrs. Williger.

Sarah was making a fuss of carrying a large bowl of tossed salad to the table. I sat down, exchanging my orange plate for the blue one I always liked, and stared into the deep color while everyone found a place. I could hear Father come into the room and take his seat at the head of the table.

"This is my husband, Dr. Hoffman. Mr. Williger and Mrs. Williger."

"Howdy," Rosie boomed.

"Pleased to meet you," said Mrs. Williger.

"Good to meet you, too."

Father was holding out his suddenly small hand to greet Rosie's hairy bear-like fist.

"And you haven't met my oldest, Efa," Mother was saying.

I smiled weakly.

"Howdy Miss," Mr. Williger's red freckled face seemed to crinkle as he nodded.

"Hi."

"Hello, honey," Mrs. Williger said, and delicately spread a paper napkin over her starched dress.

"I don't know if you folks are used to giving the good Lord His due." Rosie's booming voice made the dining room seem small.

"Rosie means saying grace," Mrs. Williger explained weakly.

"I'm afraid you've joined a secular family," Father smiled with amusement as he helped himself to meat.

"Well, if I understand you right, that's just fine with me. 'Course I don't know about Mary Ellen here."

"No, no, he doesn't want to pray," Mrs. Williger said hurriedly, with her china doll smile.

"If you'd like to, you should do it," offered Mother.

"No, really, that's just fine," said Mrs. Williger, glancing at her husband. "Rosie'll be just as glad for the break."

The food was still being passed around and everyone was beginning to eat. Except for Mrs. Williger and myself, people seemed to be very hungry or in a great rush. I could hear Mr. Williger chewing, and then he sucked the food from the cracks in his teeth. What would it have been like with the Johnsons sitting around our table?

"It's good," Father nodded reassuringly at Mother, and lay his hand momentarily on hers.

"Uhm, real delicious," Mr. Williger agreed loudly, and I wondered if he was a little hard of hearing from working on noisy trains all day.

Mother leaned across the table to urge another helping of meat onto his plate. "Here, I know you can eat more. A big man like you!" she laughed excitedly.

"Don't mind if I do!"

Jolie and Sarah were giggling and kicking each other's feet under the table.

Mrs. Williger delicately wiped her mouth. "Dr. Hoffman, we know the trouble we must be. We thought we might be able to figure out something else for a time." Suddenly I realized why she smiled as she did: she was missing a front tooth.

Father cleared his throat awkwardly.

"Really, doctor. I think Rosie wanted to tell you, didn't you Rosie?" she looked hopefully to her husband.

"Well, I sure didn't relish spending a month or two in a church," Mr. Williger said. "It was already two weeks, wasn't it Mary Ellen? More than enough time to get me into heaven, as I used to say to the folks there. And there were some still living there when we left!"

"Rosie's not a church man," Mrs. Williger smiled sadly, and her tiny gold cross gleamed at him.

"No, sir, I'm like you. I can't say as I would go into one of those places of my own will, if you know what I mean? No harm meant," Rosie laughed, and gave a little man-to-man nod in Father's direction.

Father thumped the table and smiled: his guests were entertaining him just as he wanted.

"Many people are spoiled these days, and they don't appreciate what they've got." Mother put down her fork.

Mary Ellen puckered her mouth worriedly; she seemed afraid that Mother was about to criticize her husband's lack of respect for a church, particularly one that had saved them.

"Some people think children need a room of their own. But that's just American fashion. When I was a child, we had a very nice home, very nice." Mother's eyes glistened behind her glasses. "But there were seven children, and no child had a room alone. If there is no difficulty, I let my children have whatever is the fashion in America. Not that I approve. But I couldn't allow one to be a little princess while whole families live crowded together in basements. That's just not right."

My cheeks flamed at the little speech, clearly meant for me.

"Efa and I went to a church." Mother's eyes were on me, and then she turned away. "The people in the church did what they could to make things comfortable. But it's no way to live, so many families crowded together. And my children must learn to share. If they live like princesses when they're young, how will they adjust if something bad happens to them?"

The fork I had been holding dropped from my fingers and clanged loudly against my blue plate.

"Your mom said you gave us your room, so we sure do want to thank you," Mrs. Williger turned to me cautiously, and her sweet pained smile and tiny cross were beamed on me.

I tried to smile back.

"But we're not princesses," Sarah was saying brightly. "We don't usually get seconds of meat, or have so many things on the table." She glanced impishly around the table.

"Sarah!" Mother started to reprimand her, but her face changed in midstream and she burst out laughing.

Mr. Williger chuckled, and Mrs. Williger fell into a squeaky choked laugh that exposed the black hole where the tooth should have been.

I looked over at Father. A dry smile played on his lips. From his vantage of miles away, he was finding the toy dinner pleasantly amusing. He hadn't even noticed how Mother had betrayed me.

"You got a nice daughter here." Mr. Williger jabbed Sarah's arm playfully, then turned to me. "Both of them, real nice."

I glued my eyes to my plate, grateful to be across the table, out of reach of his arm. The one thing Mr. Williger didn't seem was a phoney, but he had no reason so far to call me nice.

"Pretty too!"

"I'm afraid Sarah's right," Mother laughed. "Tomorrow night, if you don't object, we will eat more simply. Maybe even macaroni."

"Oh, please, for heavens sakes, don't go to any trouble!" Mrs. Williger smiled a closed-mouth pathetic smile. "Anyway, Rosie'll be out working extra shifts most nights. I myself don't eat much, and Jolie she'll eat just about anything. Won't you, honey?"

Jolie wrinkled her pug nose and kicked Sarah under the table.

"Yup, we sure can use the extra money, with all we got to build over again from scratch. Also, there's what we got to replace. You can't imagine what all you've bought over the years until you have to go out and buy it all over again," boomed Mr. Williger. "But the flood tore up them railroad ties like pretzels, so I guess I can be thankful there's enough work."

"So you'll be all tied up," Father said ponderously, and grinned at himself.

"Excuse me?"

"I made a pun. Railroad ties—tied up? Nothing important." Father rocked against his chair.

"We too had to start all over," Mother told them. "I left with a small cardboard suitcase. David had the leather one that's still in the attic. 'How lucky!' I laughed with him, 'that we only recently married. That way we don't have so much to lose.' But David was more upset. He had so many books. He tried to sell them to a dealer in a secondhand book store, but the dealer wasn't supposed to buy anything from Jews."

Father leaned forward, interrupting. "Is repairing the railroad tracks then your regular job?" I knew he was embarrassed by Mother talking about the war.

"I'm what they call general maintenance," said Mr. Williger, giving Mother a friendly but confused nod. "Tracks, some car work. I don't do much on the engines."

Mother gave Father a cautious glance, then turned to Mr. Williger. "*Ach!* And now you work sixteen hours a day? That's not fair."

"I don't reckon fair has much to do with anything these days, Ma'am."

"But you bring along your meals so that you eat healthy food."

"Oh, he gets his meat and potatoes, wherever he is," Mrs. Williger assured Mother.

"I can make you food to take in a paper sack. It's so expensive, in a restaurant!"

"Now, Ma'am—"

"At home, we always eat meat every night," Jolie announced, looking defiantly at her Mother. "That's 'cause we killed Big Joe, and we was still eating him when the flood come."

Mrs. Williger tittered. "Big Joe, he was a cow we raised until we had him slaughtered last spring." She patted her red mouth with her napkin. "The worst thing was, when the electricity lines come down, we lost every bit of the meat in our freezer. Why, there must have been a good quarter of Big Joe left, wouldn't you say, Rosie? We just couldn't get it anywhere safe, what with everything else we had to do."

"We lost a lot more than Big Joe. All the chickens! But we was lucky the way we come through—compared to some." Mr. Williger belched.

"It's so awful what nature can do sometimes," Mother looked straight past me.

"I know. I thank the Lord for my blessings each night," said Mrs. Williger, raising her pencil-thin brows, "though it's hard to imagine people with more taken from them."

"Now, there's people with even more taken, don't you worry. You saw them right in front of your eyes at the church. And I got my job—which is more than a lot of them." Mr. Williger leaned back in his seat. "Anyway, sure is nice having a large family like this. Both me and Mary Ellen come from big families. I would have had a big one myself. But Mary Ellen, here, is so tiny we was lucky she could carry Jolie the whole way. And then," he winked at Father, "she ain't interested too often, you know."

"I love large families too," Mother agreed enthusiastically. "We had seven children at home in Vienna."

Amusement tilted the corners of Father's mouth as he thumped the table with his fist.

"David does that sometimes," Mother quickly laughed.

Sarah and Jolie were making eyes at each other like two bratty sisters.

"Eva usually practices the violin before or right after supper," Father announced, and once more thumped the table. "She will spare you the concert tonight. But I'm afraid that starting tomorrow both you and she will have to bear with it." He pushed his chair back from the table and smiled at me, pleased with himself.

I thrust my plate away, not caring that as it slid my uneaten peas went flying over the table.

"Well, isn't that interesting? Rosie, isn't that interesting?" Mary Ellen appealed to her husband. "We sure never did expect all this, now did we?"

*T*he day was hot but dry and with the help of the little fan the air circulated through my attic room and kept me sleeping late. I stayed in bed a few minutes after waking. The night before, the Williger's first evening had continued loud and boisterous, and everyone seemed to enjoy themselves. Father had sat at his beloved piano and, pulling out a book of American folk tunes, he'd coaxed Jolie and Sarah into singing folk songs to his accompaniment. After a while, I'd gone upstairs, but even from the third floor I could hear the high screech of "The cabin never leaks when it doesn't rain," which they all found very funny. Now I seemed to hear dance band music filtering up through the floor boards in a disturbing but pleasant way. I burrowed my head under my pillow at the thought of facing all the people. But when my bladder began to press, I pulled on my shorts and halter and went down.

Once on the second floor, I could hear a radio coming from . . . yes, that's what it was now: the Williger's bedroom. The door was ajar, and I quietly peeked in. A white chenille bedspread covered the large bed, and a pearl handled hair brush and manicure set and several bottles of perfume were laid out neatly on a cream lace shawl on top of the bureau next to a small plastic radio. Someone had also spread a white lace table cloth over the soggy boxes that stood against the wall. The room looked as fussy and cluttered as when it was Grandmother's, and it smelled like a field of lilies of the valley in high bloom. The whole effect seemed odd for a room a man slept in too, especially since Rosie was so bulky and tough and probably came home from the railroad dirty with grease. A pink light glowed from the radio, and a dance band was playing a romantic bouncy tune. I did a step or two, imitating grownup dancers I had seen in the movies. Maybe when I grew up I would escape all my worries and be like Ginger Rogers twirling through a wonderland of grand pianos.

Sounds of scrambling broke through the music, then Sarah's rolling giggle and Jolie's sharp laugh. "Don't."—"Don't do it to *me*."—"No, *you* stop it!" I went to the bathroom and turned the doorknob.

"Shh!" came Sarah's voice, followed by more scrambling and hushed laughter.

I knocked on the door. "Let me in."

"Be quiet!" They were talking to each other.

I knocked again, louder. "Let me in. I've got to go to the bathroom!"

"Hurry, we have to clean this up," Sarah was whispering.

"It don't matter. But let's not let her in!"

I could picture Jolie's puffy freckled face. "Come on, you guys! Let me in," I demanded, banging with my fist. Sarah's giggle had turned frightened. "Let me in," I said. "I have to pee."

"We can't right now," Sarah squealed, and I could hear one of them hitting the other.

"I'm going to get Mother, if you don't let me in."

"We can't, that's all," laughed Jolie.

They didn't sound as if they were in the bathtub, but I couldn't imagine what they were doing. "What's going on in there?"

"Nothing—!"

I gave the door a hard kick. "Hurry up, or I'm getting Mother." The bathroom was suddenly quiet. I put my eye to the keyhole, but all I could see was a slice of Sarah's plump knee against the bathmat. Straightening, I kicked again. "Okay for you!" The pressure was growing steadily in my groin and even stuffing my head. It wasn't fair, what they were doing! You couldn't monopolize the bathroom! I marched downstairs, holding myself tensely, but making sure my steps returned ominous sounds to the bathroom. Never had Sarah locked the bathroom door on me. This was all Jolie's work! If this was how it was going to be...

"Mother!" I called, as I reached the bottom step. I made a circle, through the kitchen, into the dining room, back through the living room. I yelled down into the basement, "Mother!"

"Mother!" I shouted, leaning out the back door.

"Here, *süsse*, we're in the side yard."

Blinking at the blinding sun, I went around the house. Mother and Mrs. Williger were on their knees laying out table cloths like flower petals around a moldy little night table. The yellow and white cloths were blotched with dank green and smelled of mildew.

"Sarah and Jolie locked themselves in the bathroom and won't let me in," I complained, squeezing one leg tightly in front of the other.

Mother stood up and surveyed the table cloths. "Did you ask them to open it?" she asked.

"Of course I did! And I have to go very badly."

"Oh, dear," Mary Ellen Williger sighed, and brushed off her starchy pink dress. "Times that Jolie gets something into her head, you just can't hardly do nothing with her."

Mother looked with surprise at Mrs. Williger. "Do you want to tell your daughter to open the door for Efa?" she asked politely.

"I don't know if it'll do much good. When Jolie puts her mind to a thing—" She stood up and straightened the little plastic belt at her waist.

"Ma! I have to go to the bathroom."

Mrs. Williger was tiptoeing around the cloths to go back towards the house. Her dark hair shone in the sunlight, but she already looked defeated.

Mother shook her head, watching Mrs. Williger. "Should I go?"

"Well, maybe you might better. If her father were home, he'd get out the switch. She don't listen to me too good." Mrs. Williger trailed behind us until she reached the kitchen, where she stopped before the sink and carefully washed her hands.

"Why can't Mrs. Williger get Jolie to mind?" I whispered as we trotted up the stairs.

"*Ich weiss nicht,*" Mother said, shaking her head in warning that she wouldn't put up with nonsense. "Please open up immediately. Efa has to use the bathroom. Anyway, we don't lock bathroom doors in our house."

There were frightened giggles in the bathroom, and the lock snapped open. Sarah's curtained face appeared in the crack of the door. Mother pushed in the door, yanking Sarah's arm as she strode into the bathroom. The floor was littered with open jars of old and new shoe polish, but no shoes were to be seen. Mother grabbed Jolie's freckled arm with her other hand. Now she had one girl in each. Jolie was giggling in a nervous nasty way, but Mother's fingers were digging red marks in her flesh.

"I want you to go into your room while Efa uses the bathroom. She will tell you when she's through, and then you will come in and put all this shoe polish away."

Sarah lowered her head sorrowfully as Mother released her.

I went into the bathroom and sat on the toilet. The rack above the sink was already cluttered with the Williger's toothbrushes, toothpaste, razorblades and shaving cream. On the floor all around me lay the open shoe polish jars. I hadn't known we had so many: brown, blue, oxblood, neutral, black. The whole bathroom was heavy with the sweet odor of wax. I flushed the toilet, washed my face and hands, and brushed my teeth for the day. On a hunch, I opened the bathroom closet door. Half a dozen pairs of shoes had been thrown onto the floor and lay all topsy turvy. Some looked like Sarah's, except that they were no longer their original colors: red was blue and white was brown. Shutting the closet door, I marched into Sarah's room.

"I saw what you did," I announced. "You're going to be in real trouble."

"We can clean it up," sang out Jolie. The two were still giggling as they waited on Sarah's bed.

I turned from the room and tramped back downstairs. Mother now stood at the front door, speaking through the screen to Mrs. Rogers, who had on her black toreador pants and an aqua silk scarf tied over her pin curls.

"I was just afraid she might ruin both her table and her cloths." Mrs. Rogers fussed with some news clippings she held in her hand. "I saw you all lay them out, so I thought I'd better come right over and tell you." Ill at ease, she was pretending to be in a hurry.

"Hi, Mrs. Rogers—Ma," I said.

"Just a minute," Mother waved me on. "Why don't you come and talk to Mrs. Williger." She opened the screen door.

Mrs. Rogers tilted her head to one side, caught off guard at the idea of entering our house, and with sudden determination let herself in. "Hi, honey," she said to me, then turned to Mother, "I hope you don't mind me interfering. But I was saving those little items from the paper." She glanced down at the newspaper clippings. "You know, in case they might come in handy. So I realized when I saw that table, I had one here says that, you know, you're not supposed to put wet furniture right in the sun."

"*Ach*, that's very kind of you."

"Ma!" I said, and wished I hadn't interrupted.

Mother turned to me. "Did you go to the bathroom?"

"Yes, but—"

Mrs. Rogers was offering the little clippings.

"No, you should give them to Mrs. Williger," said Mother, pointing to the kitchen where Mary Ellen Williger stood in the shadows. "Mrs. Williger, this is my neighbor, Mrs. Rogers."

"Hi," Mrs. Rogers flashed a glamorous smile and adjusted her aqua scarf. "I'm Betty. Mrs. Hoffman here always stays real formal, but you can call me Betty."

It was strange, I thought, that Mrs. Rogers had never said that to me. Betty—the name felt awkward on my lips.

"My name's Mary Ellen," Mrs. Williger came into the living room to join us. She patted at her hair, which already lay as smooth as a bathing cap around her flat face.

"I saw your night table out there in the side yard," Mrs. Rogers began. "I was just telling Mrs. Hoffman that I had some clippings out of the *Capital* about cleaning and drying things from the flood."

"You should call me Leah," Mother said stiffly. "That is my first name." She wanted to be like the other women but didn't know how.

I went into the kitchen and poured myself a bowl of cold cereal and milk. Mother would be furious if she knew about the shoes, but I didn't want to confuse her when she was finally trying to be friends with American women. I brought my bowl and spoon into the living room and sat on the couch. Mrs. Rogers was showing Mary Ellen Williger a clipping that said wood should be dried in the shade to prevent cracking. Then Mrs. Williger looked at one that recommended several possible solutions for taking mildew out of cloth. Mother must have given up a little, for she had begun busying herself by dusting surfaces around the two women.

"Javelle water, that sounds the best." Mrs. Rogers pulled out a package of cigarettes from her pants pocket and glanced uncertainly at Mother.

"It's real kind of you to bring over all this information," said Mary Ellen Williger. "Isn't it, Mrs. Hoffman?"

Mother looked up from her rag. "Mrs. Rogers is the woman I told you about who added sheets to my pile when I brought them to that church."

Mrs. Williger smiled weakly, exposing the dark space in her mouth. "Let's see, I guess I better go out to the store and get the washing soda and bleaching powder." She pursed her lips as she studied the recipe for Javelle water.

Mother glanced over Mrs. Williger's shoulder at the clipping. "I have a strainer you can use," she said, "and of course a big pot."

"The IGA's just across Sixth. If you want, I'll walk you over," said Mrs. Rogers. "The first time and all, you might want company. I always do." She had her makeup on and even her pincurl scarf wasn't stopping her from beaming her Hollywood charm on Mrs. Williger.

"That'd be real kind, I'd be much obliged." Mary Ellen Williger suddenly fell into her hiccup laugh. "Oh my, here we are talking about how to do everything right, and my night table is still standing out there in the sun."

"I'll get it for you." Mother lept toward the front door.

"Now, you let me get it, Mrs. Hoffman," Mary Ellen Williger said, and turned to Mrs. Rogers. "This lady is something! She won't let you do hardly a thing for yourself. Before you can even think what you need she's already doing it."

Mother had stopped short to see if she would be held back, but now she closed the screen door behind her.

Mrs. Rogers pulled a cigarette from her package with her long painted fingernails. "The Hoffmans have real interesting art, don't you think?" she asked Mrs. Williger. Her eye roamed

over the small pictures and came to rest on the Negro man above
the couch as she gave an efficient strike to her match.

"I haven't had much time to look around, myself," Mrs.
Williger laughed nervously.

"There's an ashtray on the bookshelf," I told Mrs. Rogers
from my perch on the green couch.

"Oh, thanks honey."

"So you people are going to stay here a while, that's real
nice," said Mrs. Rogers, dropping her match into the ashtray.
"You ought to come over and watch TV—My husband bought
me mine before he left for Korea. Eva will tell you, she likes it
a lot. Also, we got a revival meeting going on every night now.
Reverend Snyder. He's here for two weeks, and we've got a few
days left. I don't know if you read about him, but he's
internationally famous. I go over there most evenings with my
son. If you'd care to come along—"

"I went to church with Mrs. Rogers once," I said, and
suddenly my stomach felt uneasy.

"My husband usually works most evenings." Mrs. Williger
touched her throat where the golden cross glimmered. "But I
wouldn't mind coming along myself. The kind of trouble we've
had," she smiled weakly, "you can use a little help from up
there."

"Well, Reverend Snyder is real good, real good." Mrs.
Rogers inhaled with her eyes closed, then blew little white smoke
circles in the air. "My husband, he was wounded here a while
back, and then they messed him up more when they tried to
operate. But Reverend Snyder fixed me up just fine. He can take
just about anything in your life and practically make you see it
as a blessing in disguise."

Mrs. Williger tilted her head like a little dog afraid of a
reprimand. "I don't know if Mrs. Hoffman told you. Our house
ain't fit to live in. My husband, Rosie, he's been going back
nights after work to get one thing and another," she said.
"There's still a foot of water everywhere. My best china cabinet
is packed in mud. I can't face the place. The city condemned it.
Anyway, I worry about Rosie. He oughtn't to be going there
alone after dark."

"Reverend Snyder can put you in fine shape," Mrs. Rogers repeated, nodding, and flicked an ash. Mrs. Williger seemed to give her extra confidence, or else it was the minister she had been to see. "I mean, the man knows what's gone on in this town. He's talked to city officials. He's been out personally to visit people's homes. But he can find reasons for what happens, and he can make you see things in a different way."

"I'm just hoping we don't have to move." Mrs. Williger looked down at her small chicken-bone hands. "I'm crossing my fingers we can fix up the place."

"It's bad," Mrs. Rogers agreed. "I'm just lucky, what with my husband half way across the world in Korea with shrapnel still in his knee."

"Mother's at the door," I said quietly from my seat, starting to rise to help her.

"Oh dear me!" Mary Ellen Williger exclaimed, and rushed to the screen door. Mother stood on the porch, her arms around the night table piled high with folded cloths. "Now Mrs. Hoffman, you really shouldn't have done all that. I could have gone out later and picked up the table cloths."

Mother brought in the table and set it down near the piano bench. "I don't think the sun hurt it yet." She knelt and examined the cracked moldy wood.

"Now see, like with this night table," said Mrs. Rogers, flicking her ashes. "Reverend Snyder could make you understand, let's say it did get cracked in the sun. He could make you see how it was time in your life to buy a brand new night table. But you would really understand and feel good."

Mother's eyes widened in disbelief as she looked over at Mrs. Rogers.

"It looks just fine to me," Mrs. Williger said to Mother. She seemed confused as she turned away from Mother to give Mrs. Rogers a helpless smile.

Mother stood up, her hands on her sturdy hips. She wiped her forehead, and I could see her quietly sigh; but she said cheerfully, "I need coffee, would you like to have some hot coffee with me?"

"Oh my, I just had a cup before coming over." Mrs. Rogers stamped out her cigarette and looked to see what Mrs. Williger would do.

"Mrs. Hoffman can't stop doing nice things for people," Mary Ellen Williger laughed ambiguously.

Dance music was wafting through the house from upstairs. Mother never allowed radio music except when Father turned it on to listen to a concert or the Metropolitan Opera. I could see her getting into a bad mood that would make her tense and jumpy. "Ma," I insisted. "Ma, I have something to tell you," and watched her turn to me with relief on her perspiring face.

S ometimes it seemed that the Willigers had begun living with us long before that summer, or that, even with them there, everything went on as before. I had to practice in the evenings, Father played the piano or read his books, there were the three meals at regular times each day, though with more people at a crowded table. I had almost forgotten how it felt to close the door and snuggle down inside my pink lace room. Or to think about one thing after another in a quiet way. Yet I knew people were changing, if not before my eyes, then beneath my dusty attic floor. I no longer had Sarah to talk to when I needed to test my thoughts. It seemed I no longer had Mother or Father either, and that they didn't really have each other. Except for Sarah and Jolie, who raced through the neighborhood, cutting across lawns and jumping over hedges to Jolie's piercing Woody Woodpecker call until long after dark, the house was busy with people who were tucked in their own shells. Some days I longed for Mrs. Johnson to come just so we could talk.

One evening I was roaming the first floor, uncertain where exactly to spend my time. From a distance, I watched Mother sew. I fingered the keys of Father's piano, went into the kitchen, and thumbed through the day's newspaper lying on the table. Then, through the gauzy white dining room curtain, I peered out at Father and Mordecai, who sat side-by-side in deck chairs near the sumac bushes. They were talking quietly, only nodding at each other from time to time. Father carved at the overgrown grass with the side of his heavy sandal.

"You should leave them alone." Mother glanced over from her sewing. She was being especially cautious, because Father had snapped at her earlier for nothing at all.

Above the men, high pink clouds passed like fluorescent lace over a graying sky. Father seemed to be explaining something in a low angry voice. I backed away from the window and went to stand beside Mother. She was ripping out the hem of a plaid dress of Jolie's in preparation for resewing it a few inches lower. She had taken sewing lessons in Vienna, in case she needed to find work in her new country. A pair of ripped shorts and a pastel green dress of Mrs. Williger's lay by her side. Mary Ellen and Betty, as they now asked for each other on the phone, had gone off together to see *From Here to Eternity.*

"I don't see why you're doing that," I said.

Mother gave a hard little laugh. "You heard, she was going to throw away these clothes because they didn't fit."

"Mrs. Williger has a right to throw her own clothes away."

"You have a point," Mother said, in a weak voice that made me afraid to press the argument.

I moved away from Mother, wandered through the kitchen and onto the back porch. Father and Mordecai might not want me, but I wouldn't stop myself in advance from going outside. Opening the back door slowly to prevent it from creaking, I let myself out and sat down silently on the back steps.

Clouds raced southward, like great silver birds, and the pink had sunk to the horizon. The air was filled with the high drone of crickets. The two men sat low in their canvas deck chairs and gazed over the Cotter's backyard and beyond, downhill toward Sixth. Mordecai looked dark and frail as he sat with his legs crossed in the deck chair; in one hand he cupped his pipe, which he cleaned with a tiny silver spoon as he talked. Way on the other side of the next yard, the Cotter children were catching fireflies in canning jars. They played secretively together, as if hiding their game from outsiders' eyes. The other morning, Sarah and Jolie had slipped through a space in the fence and tried to tease them into playing, but they had turned aside and finally disappeared into the house. Perhaps because they went to Catholic school during the winter, they didn't think they had to be friends with other kids in the neighborhood during the summer months. Yet they could choose, Mother said, to come to our school along with everyone else. And they could live on our street. It wasn't the same as with Mayella and her brothers.

After a while I crossed the lawn and sat on the chilled grass at the foot of Father's chair. Mordecai had kicked off his shoes, and his stockinged feet were like long black tongues. A mosquito alighted on my thigh, and I quickly swatted it, but it had already left its sting.

"I just don't see why you even spoke to them," Mordecai was saying.

"I live in America. I try not to assume that I'm on the other side from the law," Father laughed.

"That's rather naive, especially if you're taking the side of the Negroes, or someone who's fighting for the rights of Negroes."

"It may be, but I couldn't imagine anything about Helene that would make her more than a pure Kansas girl," said Father, and I felt his hand gently touch my shoulder.

"You don't know what those people will do with whatever you say."

"I told you, when I realized what they were driving at—that they were trying to make joining the NAACP the same as being a Communist—I told them to be on their way."

"I guess it just surprises me. It seems part of your new attitude of not caring."

"You yourself have a strange attitude," Father said roughly. "Whenever we disagree you think I don't care. Is yours perhaps the only caring point of view?"

"I think there are other views than mine that are caring. Yours, these days, don't strike me as particularly so."

"Well, I'll tell you one more uncaring aspect of my opinion," said Father, whose voice was again raised in the quiet night. "I think Helene and her people have sent that suit down an unfortunate track. They want to argue that segregation is wrong because it makes children feel bad and stunts their education. If it didn't, would they think segregation was right? Really, I can't understand that kind of crap. Imagine using that with the ghettoes of Europe. It would have been ridiculous! Everyone knew that Jewish education and culture were thriving. But that didn't make emancipation irrelevant. Doesn't anyone here believe in justice for its own sake?"

"You have a point," Mordecai said slowly.

Father pounded the arm of his deck chair. "And if the Negro children don't do better in the white schools, will they say that integration has failed?"

"You're right," Mordecai said again.

"Will they ignore the prejudice of white teachers and say that Negro children can't learn as well as whites?" Father pushed his point.

"I guess my complaint is that you use that very excellent insight to lacerate yourself and others with the futility of what we want to do. It's as though everything is condemned to failure from the start. So anyone who tries to help is being blind and stupid. Nothing really matters."

"I think some things matter, but I *don't* believe anyone, myself included, is making wonderful leaps forward to a better world."

Mordecai sucked his pipe and the sweet smell of his tobacco filled the air. "Well, that's what I mean. You make it a general principle: you know, no one has any real power to—"

"I think I had limited power with the FBI, which I took. I don't think I have much more power than that most of the time," Father interrupted, and there was cruel bitterness in his voice.

"The smart-talking Jew, confusing them with your words!" Mordecai laughed.

Father leaned his head against the canvas and looked up at the thinning clouds. The first star had come out and shone a bright warning against the crepuscular sky.

"It was you who used to argue that we all chose our destinies—even with Hitler," Mordecai said. "It was such a good way of thinking."

"Except in the most limited sense, I now think that's pure arrogance." Father kicked the grass with his heel.

I didn't like the tone Father was taking. I was afraid they would grow more nasty with each other, or suddenly get into a fight again. The mosquito had left its swollen nodule, which I had been scratching, and now the scraped head of the bump began to bleed and the itch turned sharp and almost sweet. I could make the sting so strong it blotted out their voices.

"I suppose I am bitter," Father was saying. "I had wanted to do something important. Whatever that means. I still have ideas, but they seem like short-lived enthusiasms. Then I see the huge effort someone like Helene puts forth. For what?" He gave an ironic laugh as I smeared the blood against my thigh. "Great art. Helping humankind. What does anyone achieve? I don't even speak of myself: sitting here amidst my pleasant, if ordinary family, in some provincial town." He swept his hand toward the house.

"I think you severely underestimate what will happen with the suit," Mordecai said, blowing his spicy pipe smoke into the distance. "I could also argue against your view of yourself. As for me, well. I have trouble enough without . . ."

"So I'm both cynical and naive," said Father. "You don't paint me very attractively."

"I'm not finding you attractive in this respect. I find you exasperating."

The Cotter kids were fading in a dusky haze and then their mother called them indoors. A light had come on inside our house where Mother sat sewing. With Father so miserable, I almost wished I had stayed inside with her. I dabbed some spit on my mosquito bite. I wanted to reach out my hand to him, but I was only ordinary now.

"I heard a joke from a patient," Father said, and thumped on the wooden arm of his deck chair. "Two Jews are walking down the street. Behind them two Gentiles make anti-Semitic remarks as they walk. 'We should do something to stop them,' says one of the Jews. 'What can we do?' asks the other. 'They're together and we're alone.'"

Mordecai chuckled. "At least you see your problem."

There was silence for a few minutes, and somewhere in the distance I could hear Jolie's cackling Woodpecker call. Father's joke had made me think of Mother and me walking with our shopping bags toward the church. Or of Mrs. Johnson as she came slowly up our street all alone on hot shimmery mornings.

"Look, if you believe in the new direction of your work, then congratulations," Father said roughly. "I just don't see it. I think you're fumbling like everyone else. One day psychoanalysis will be looked back on as another false enthusiasm that gave faint hope while it lasted."

"The long view, from which nothing has meaning," said Mordecai.

"Maybe."

"I'm surprised you can help anyone with your attitude. No choice. No meaning."

Father laughed. "Perhaps that is exactly the adjustment we're lacking."

Mordecai sucked his pipe.

"Anyway, you know I don't feel I help anyone much these days."

"Too bad."

Above me, Mordecai's and Father's bodies had become luminous silhouettes. Father brushed back his wild hair, and his hand was like a black post against the sky. I shivered and slapped my arms. Their conversation had made me itchy and upset.

"Maybe I'm avoiding my own depression—and also doubts," Mordecai said. "God knows, I have my own personal sorrows. But there must be some higher meaning."

"Ha!" Father said.

"Not even in music, eh? Anyway, I really can't stand to be around you when you're like this."

"Then don't," said Father. "You have every right to go your own way. You have been recently, anyway."

"Do I hear resentment?"

"Also relief."

"I feel sad," Mordecai said quietly, feeling for his shoes in the grass. "We're friends, at least we have been. We had a long common past over there, in middle Europe."

"That we did, and do."

The lights of a car spread across the bushes by the garage and the hoarse sound of its motor jangled the night. I watched the red glow of its tail lights as it went on up the alley. Everything seemed ended if Mordecai and Father parted without being reconciled. Yet they sat without moving, and the black air was a hard rock between them. I let the tears silently glaze my cheeks.

After a time, I said, my voice cracking, "I'm going inside now."

Father lightly touched my shoulder, then turned to Mordecai, "I guess we also should stop."

O ver the next few days I would sit on my attic bed, going over fragments of Father's and Mordecai's talk. Although Father never troubled to disguise his gloom or worry, he was not one to volunteer information about his more private thoughts. And now, as in the cold of winter when Grandmother had died, he drifted further into his books and music and his gloomy face showed he was in another troubled world. It was embarrassing how sometimes he didn't even notice when Mary Ellen Williger came into the room or Rosie talked to him. Still, the silly games Sarah and Jolie played, or the plans Mother worked out to take care of Mary Ellen and Mrs. Rogers, seemed small, far away from the important event I had witnessed and was still trying to sort out. Mother always said, "Speak nicely to the police. Ask them the way if you're lost." But Father had laughed at the men who'd come to our door, and Mordecai had said that wasn't enough. I would think of the tiredness in Father's voice as he had called our family ordinary. The accusation made me sad, even angry. Though ours was the only family I had ever known, in the neighborhood and school I knew we were looked upon as strange. Of course, that strangeness wasn't there for Father—as it wasn't for me; but nothing about us seemed to give him any special meaning or joy. Father wanted something, some vague hopeful thing which Mordecai thought he himself destroyed again and again each time it came to him. If Father still lived in Vienna, would he be this way?

"What did your father and Mordecai talk about on the lawn last night?" Mother tried to sound casual, but her eyes were testy.

How could I tell her? "I can't remember," I answered, and watched her suck her teeth and return to the household tasks.

One afternoon, when Mrs. Johnson was cleaning, I turned the bend in the stairs to see Jolie alone on the living room rug. She had a box of cracker jacks and was shaking them onto the Persian rug in order to find the plastic trinket that came along inside as a free prize. I could hear the noise of the vacuum sweeper, and then it snapped off and Mrs. Johnson appeared in the room. Her face was like a beam of dark intense light inside her neat black crown of hair.

"Young lady, I just cleaned that rug," she said.

Jolie stared at Mrs. Johnson without saying anything. She popped a cracker jack into her mouth and shook more of the box onto the fresh rug.

"You heard what I said? I don't clean no rug a second time in one week." Her dark face seemed to drain of its color.

I hung back at the banister, afraid to interfere.

Mrs. Johnson took out a handkerchief and wiped her high forehead. She was standing about four feet away from Jolie, and her black eyes were on the cracker jacks. "Miss, did you hear what I said?"

Jolie glanced up at me, and an odd smile played on her lips. Then she turned to Mrs. Johnson. "I ain't taking no orders from a Nigger," she said, and began slowly to eat the spilled cracker jacks.

A shudder ran through Mrs. Johnson's thin body and for an instant she seemed to rise, and then her sleeves sagged from her bony shoulders and she disappeared into the dining room. I heard the whir of the vacuum sweeper being snapped on again. A chair scratched the floor as it was moved away from the table, and back. A hot tremor had pinned me to the spot. Jolie was calmly and methodically eating her cracker jacks. She seemed to have forgotten that anyone else was in the room. She poked her fingers in her teeth to remove the sticky popcorn. Wool from the carpet stuck to a cracker jack, and she blew it away before popping it into her mouth. A hard thickness filled my throat; I wanted to throw myself at Mrs. Johnson, to ask her forgiveness, and to tear Jolie's eyes out. Feeling too crazy where I was, I opened the front door and went outside.

The sky was a cloudless dark blue above the arching trees. Not the slightest breeze stirred the branches, even the birds were utterly still. The women had pulled the shades of their windows as they did every day now to protect their houses from the afternoon heat. A car was parked here and there along the street, but nobody was in any of them. It was as if everyone had died and or gone away. The tremor still moved up and down inside me and I was finding it hard to swallow. I could hear Jolie's, "I ain't taking no orders from a Nigger," and smell the sickly caramel of the cracker jacks.

At the corner, I sat on the mound of grass and watched the cars go by on Sixth Street. Last summer, Sarah and I had rested for hours on this very knoll. We would count the cars: Studebakers, Edsels, Hudsons, Chevrolets, or Pontiacs. The first to get ten or twenty of the lucky make won. Once, too, nearly every week, I had accompanied Grandmother across Sixth, behind the Shell station, to the beauty parlor where I had read all the new comics while Marilyn Sue's mother washed Grandmother's gray hair and then pulled my chair next to hers as she sat under the dryer and we studied a ladies' magazine. But this summer it had rained for so terribly long, and the Willigers had come to live in her room, and everything had changed. I wanted to redo what had happened with Jolie inside, yet my refusing mind turned to stone whenever I even pictured our living room.

How would I be able to talk to Mrs. Johnson after what I had seen? I had been wrong, I knew, just to stand there.

Suddenly the blue top of the bus crawled up the hill, shimmering in the heat, and I realized it was Father for whom I had been waiting. A block away, when it was in full view, the bus stopped to take on a mother and child. I jumped down onto the sidewalk to await Father. But the bus was dark inside and, though I could see bodies moving toward the front door, he wasn't among them.

Back on the knoll, I picked at the grass and imagined myself so small that I could lie under a single blade or make it form a tent over my head. To walk across somebody's lawn would take more than a day.

"Hullo, Eva!" It was Father's voice. He had a newspaper and a book tucked under his arm. I hadn't even noticed him coming up the street; he must have walked part way home.

Jumping into his outstretched arms, it was as if life had sprung back into the day! Then I glanced up at his face on which the lines of his cheeks were tired and drawn. Up close, he had a sour sweaty smell from wearing his suit in the summer heat. "Daddy," I said, leaning into his damp arm. "Daddy, Mrs. Johnson is here today."

"Uhm, yah. She comes on Tuesday?" He lifted his folded newspaper and studied a headline.

"Daddy."

"Yah?"

"Daddy? Are you okay?"

"Yes," he smiled dimly. He didn't seem present enough to help with my troubles.

"Jolie wasn't very nice to Mrs. Johnson," I began, ashamed of my cautious phrasing, but afraid to let out the whole terrible story.

"That's too bad." He started to tuck the paper under his arm to give me his attention, but the newspaper pulled at him and he took another glance.

"Really," I said.

"Where's your Mother?" He looked at me, but his mind was far away.

"I don't know. Daddy," I ventured, "She said *Nigger*."

"Uhm."

I wasn't sure he had heard. "*Nigger*. She said, 'I don't take orders from a *Nigger*.'" I repeated the words fearfully, for in running them over my tongue they seemed to cover me with dangerous slime.

"That doesn't sound very nice," he agreed distractedly.

"Nice!" What had he heard?

"Why didn't you say something?"

I looked down at the pavement moving like a grainy ribbon beneath my feet. "I don't know."

"You should speak up, you know."

"I know.—But we can't have someone in our house who talks like that. We can't, we just can't!" I cried out. "Somebody better do something."

"Eva," Father glanced down again at his paper.

"They have to leave, they just have to get out of here!"

"You're not being reasonable."

"What's reasonable!" Could anyone say anything they wanted, I wondered—and in our very house?

"I'm afraid they'll be here for a while."

I waited at the edge of the dining room while Father went to apologize to Mrs. Johnson, who stood at the ironing board, sprinkling clothes.

"It ain't the first time," she told him without looking up.

"Maybe. But it will be the last in our house," he said angrily.

When he had gone upstairs, I went up to her cautiously and put my arm around her slim waist.

"You think my children want to go to school with folks like that?" She looked at me with blazing eyes.

I shook my head dully and dropped my arm to my side. "I don't know how to talk to Jolie," I confessed with shame.

"Psst!" she hissed, and touched a wet finger to the hot iron.

As the sun began to pale in the long cool of evening, Jolie and Sarah and Bobby Rogers set up a baseball game in the backyard. Bobby had brought over his special autographed catcher's mitt and Jolie, who owned a softball and bat her Father had given her for Christmas, chose herself to be first up at bat. I should have stayed away if I couldn't talk to Jolie, but something drew me to join in. Jolie was a hard hitter, and she tore around the bases like an Irish setter. She was keeping her position at bat and making the three of us race all over the backyard and scurry behind the bushes for her balls. When it was my turn to be pitcher, I tossed the ball back and forth from one hand to another the way I had seen the boys do at school.

"Hurry up!" Jolie yelled, and the broad face she turned to me was as impudent as it had been to Mrs. Johnson in the afternoon.

A wonderful fantasy came to me of smashing Jolie's pug nose with the softball. I kept tossing the ball from one hand to the other.

"Pitch it!" Bobby Rogers called out, annoyed.

I let the ball go, and it tumbled across home base.

"Foul," Jolie spat out.

I looked around the backyard. Sarah was puttering near the sumac bushes. "You'd better get in outfield by the back porch," I yelled at her.

This time I threw the ball quickly, before I could have more evil thoughts.

There was a loud crack, as if the bat had been split in two as Jolie whipped it across the base, and the ball soared high into the air.

I squinted toward the sky. If I could catch it, I would have an out on Jolie. I would show her that I knew what was what. The ball disappeared as it lofted upward and merged with the gray dusk. It was arching a little toward my right. I was afraid of catching fast balls from so high up, but I was determined not to miss Jolie's. The softball began to drop behind me. Leaping backwards, I reached for it, and felt it slap my baby finger back before it hit the ground and dribbled away.

"Aeou!" I screeched. Pain ran through me like electric jolts in jarring waves.

"What happened?" Jolie had dropped her bat and started to run to first base.

"Aeou!"

"You okay?" she veered away from first and came running toward me.

"Stay away from me!" I screamed at her.

Sarah had come up to me. "What's wrong?" she peered into my face.

"The ball snapped my baby finger back," I panted. I shook my finger to drown its wild throbbing.

"Better put cold water on it," Jolie advised from a cautious distance.

"Shut up! Don't talk to me!" I yelled back.

"She probably sprained it." Bobby Rogers cocked his head and adjusted his army cap.

As Sarah took my finger gently in her dimpled hand, I was afraid I was going to cry. "Don't," I said, drawing back. I turned to Jolie. "You have to watch what you're doing. You can't just say awful things to people!" I shouted at the top of my lungs. "Nobody's going to like you if you act like this. This is our house, you know. You have to be nice." Then, feeling the tears too close, I told Sarah, "I'm going to put some water on my finger," and ran inside.

At the kitchen sink, I turned on the cold water. The pain was already subsiding—I would have rather it stayed on. From the living room came Mother's giddy laughter. Then Rosie's deep booming voice. "You want the nail this high, up here?" I squirted the cold water hard over my finger. Where was Father? Rosie had come home early from the railroad, and Mother was using him as a handyman to repair things in the house Father would never fix. This wasn't the first time, either. The other night, with Father reading unconcernedly in the living room, Rosie had gotten up on a ladder to clear leaves from the gutter. "You don't have to hold so tight," Rosie now chuckled, and I squirted the water harder on my baby finger and felt the tears slide under my glasses onto my cheeks. "I just want you to be safe," Mother laughed a bit too loud. "If we got a good man, we should keep him!" I could hear the squeak of the ladder under Rosie's heavy feet. I turned off the faucet and quickly dried my eyes and finger. I couldn't stay in the house with Mother and Rosie like this, and I couldn't return to Jolie and the game. Slamming the back porch door loudly so that Mother would know I had been in the kitchen, I quickly went around to the side yard and onto the front sidewalk. Silently crying, I began to walk in the last faint light of day.

O n Saturday it was hot, dry and hot. For hours I stayed in my attic room where I was reading *The Secret Garden,* trying to return to that mysterious elegant world where being all alone was romantic and you could trust that the people who finally emerged would be pleasant and loving, rather than cruel. The little girl, Mary, had discovered the door to the secret garden behind the tangled vines which covered the wall, and she was beginning to dig out ancient flowers from amongst the weeds. Ben Weatherstaff, the Yorkshire gardener, had joined her. In school, Miss Woody had been able to imitate his way of speaking, as we sat listening with our eyes closed, heads on our desks. "Springtime's commin'. Cannot tha' smell it?" Little trickles of perspiration slid into my eyes, fogging up my glasses. My damp halter clung to my midriff, and the bedspread scratched and stuck where it touched my damp skin. Mother had given me a salt pill at breakfast, as she did now whenever it was hot.

The late morning sun had forced even Jolie and Sarah, who were playing war around the yard with Bobby Rogers, to come up to their room. I could hear them below me: spurts of raucous giggles broke the hot silence; then loud heavy moving sounds came up through the floor boards. They were probably rearranging their room, as they did practically every day. I longed for the cool breeze that used to flow through my pink room. With Rosie's trips to North Topeka to retrieve their soiled belongings, my old room—Grandmother's room—had become jammed with boxes and smelled of Mary Ellen Williger's sweet perfume. Their waterlogged furniture was taking over the basement as well, filling it with a mildewed odor that reached the top of the stairs by the kitchen door. I closed my eyes and imagined my room as it had been in those precious months when I had lived there. Cool, delicately pink, the wind wafting through gauze curtains, my fish swimming peacefully in the bowl by my bed. "Springtime's commin'. Cannot tha' smell it?" Opening one eye, I glanced lazily over at the fish bowl now tucked under a rafter. For a moment I didn't even see the fish. Were they behind the seaweed? A lump caught in my throat as I sighted a rim of orange at the top of the water. I stood up. Even though I had never seen dead fish, I knew they had died. They floated on their sides like golden leaves half out of water.

"No!" I cried out.

The desperation came over me all of a sudden, without warning. One minute my eyes were flooded with tears. The next, I was blindly climbing down the stairs. As I hit the cool hall of the second floor, I shut the attic door behind me. On downward I plunged, looking for Mother. Coming off the bottom stair, I was stunned to see Mother, Mary Ellen Williger and Mrs. Rogers standing around the kitchen table together, shucking corn. Corn husks lay strewn in a high mound on the table, and a crate sat on one of the chairs. In a fit of self-pity, I started for the front door with a vague determination to leave home.

"Come look dearie!" Mother called excitedly from the kitchen as she caught me going out. "Isn't this nice? Mr. Williger got all this from someone along the railroad whose crop wasn't flooded. How lucky we are to have him in the house!"

I glanced back to see her tossing away a green husk.

"Come see! We have so much we called Mrs. Rogers! Really, it's so lucky," she turned, her face lit with smiling, to Mrs. Williger. "Without you, we would never have had fresh corn this summer!"

"Well, some of it's pretty wormy," Mary Ellen Williger ignored Mother's appreciation and critically examined an ear.

"There's good ones here," Mrs. Rogers said.

I had turned toward the kitchen, hoping for somebody to notice my condition. "It's nice corn," I said weakly, still a few feet away from the door.

Now Mother seemed to see me for the first time. What's wrong with you?" She eyed me carefully, her face darkening. "Oh, you look awful, dearie! Come here."

For a brief moment I imagined the two women vanished and me resting my head against Mother's soft breast; I cried quietly with relief while she wiped my hot brow with a damp cloth. Then through my wet glasses I saw the three women standing together. They had put down their ears of corn and were looking at me like judges.

"The child's got heat stroke," exclaimed Mrs. Rogers.

"Come here, come here." Mother separated herself from the women to come towards me. "Your face is almost purple."

"You might better put some ice on her forehead," Mary Ellen Williger suggested. Beads of perspiration rested on top of her small painted mouth.

"Here, sit down," said Mother.

"It's too hot up there. My fish—" I said, dropping onto a chair. Tears were running down the inside of my glasses and making it impossible to see. I took off my glasses and let the tears flow freely, mixing with the sweat of my face.

Mrs. Williger delicately patted my forehead with the corner of her crisp apron while Mother went to the refrigerator to pull out the ice. I could smell the sweet starch of Mary Ellen Williger's apron, but I wasn't sure I liked her thin perfumed body so close to mine.

"I wish you'd move down with Jolie and Sarah," Mother said. "It's not healthy being so hot."

Mrs. Rogers handed Mother a dish cloth in which to wrap the ice.

"I feel awful," Mrs. Williger sighed and turned to Mrs. Rogers. "To think the child is making herself sick up there, on our account."

"Nonsense," Mother said. "It's her choice to stay in the attic. She could have made other arrangements."

Tears ran faster down my cheeks as I held the searing ice to my forehead. The whole house was filled with strange people, the crates and things they left behind, or the food they brought. There had been a time when Mrs. Rogers never came across the street, and now she was in our kitchen nearly every day—yet she and I barely said a word to each other. My old room, the basement, every room in the house was taken over by the Willigers. I pictured Jolie as she had sat on the living room rug with her sticky popcorn, and Mrs. Johnson's face then and later when she talked to me. The fact that I had yelled at Jolie while my baby finger stung from her ball didn't seem to help. And now my fish had died. I began to wail loudly under the icy cloth which dripped over my face.

"*Ach, süsse.*"

Mother tried to smooth the wet hairs on my forehead, but the uncomfortable warmth of her soft body was making me still hotter. I felt like crying on and on and on—until I had driven all the strangers from the house.

"Come, let's go upstairs." Mother took my sweaty hand.

"I'm going to take Betty down to the basement to show her a chest Rosie brought back, if you don't mind," said Mary Ellen Williger, giving her close-mouthed smile.

"Certainly, go ahead. I'll join you in a few minutes."

We climbed the stairs together, Mother and I. I was still wailing as loudly as I could. In Mother's and Father's room, I sat on their bed while Mother wiped my neck and arms with a wet wash cloth.

"Why did you stay up in the attic so long?" She shook her head.

I glared at her.

"Does that feel better?"

"Yes."

Mother gently lifted my T-shirt and wiped my back. The cool moisture brought to the surface pain hidden deep in my skin.

"Ouch," I whimpered.

"You can't stay up there when it's this hot. If I'd known you were in the attic, I would have asked you to come downstairs."

Why hadn't Mother known where I was? I wondered. Before the Willigers had come, she'd always been able to keep track.

"Let's move your bed down with Sarah's and Jolie's," she smiled at me.

"I'm not sleeping with them!"

"Or maybe we could move the Willigers into Sarah's room—"

"I'm not going back downstairs until the Willigers are out of the house!"

"*Ach*, you're so stubborn," Mother sighed. She sat next to me on the bed and her eyes were wet as the tears flowed down my cheeks. After a few minutes, she took off her own glasses and wiped her eyes. "*Ach*, how selfish I was! *Ganz egoistisch*. I wanted to have children for my own pleasure. But did I imagine how they would feel?"

"What?"

"Having children is selfish," Mother shook her head sadly. "In this world one almost doesn't have a right."

"Ma!" I said, not wanting to be confused by her sudden troubles.

"I had so much hope when I knew I was pregnant. To start again. But now what misery I bring!"

Mother sounded so shaky she reminded me of Lillian, and suddenly the fish floating dead on the water was so terrible that I couldn't even tell her about it. "Ma!" I cried out, "When are they going to leave?"

Mother sighed, wiped her glasses on her sundress, and put them back on. "Mr. Williger talked this morning about buying an acre of land. It's somewhere outside of town." She shook her head, forcing herself to concentrate. "That's where he and David went a couple of hours ago. He apparently can buy it for a good price. But Mrs. Williger doesn't want to leave her old neighborhood. Anyway he has to build something on the new plot before they can leave."

"Build a complete new house? That's going to take years!"

"Shh," said Mother, taking my arm. "You want them to go back to their old home?" But she looked as though she would grow teary again.

"Mrs. Williger is in the basement," I said.

"She might be back in the kitchen," Mother sniffed. "And Jolie is in the next room."

"Jolie says prejudiced things to people," I hissed.

"Efa," Mother warned.

"She does! She said *Nigger* to Mrs. Johnson."

"*Ach*!" Mother shut her eyes as if she already knew, but could not again consider, the misfortune.

"But build a whole house!"

"At least enough to live in."

$\mathcal{N}$obody had noticed the dark clouds tumble and fill the sky. Then, as the rain came spurting down and bounding off the pavement like hail, the temperature of the air suddenly dropped. Oh no! I thought, wondering if the rain would again fall endlessly and the flood begin all over. Sarah and Jolie came running inside giggling hysterically, banging the door behind them. Sarah's wet bangs hung in her eyes, and Jolie's hair had fallen out of its pigtails and stuck like reddish paste over her back and shoulders.

"Oh dear, we lost Bobby!" shrieked Jolie, wringing out her dress.

"Oops!" Sarah doubled over with glee.

"Is Roy Rogers really his uncle?" Jolie asked.

"No!" Sarah whispered conspiratorially.

"Boy, is he going to get it!"

Pushing and slapping, they made their way up the stairs.

Father came into the living room and snapped on the lamp over my chair, but I wasn't doing anything in particular that needed light.

"Did you practice?" he asked, eyeing me.

"Not yet."

"Please do then."

"Will you accompany me?"

"Not today. Sometimes you have to do it by yourself."

Father walked out of the room, and I could hear him lowering the window in the dining room. The mayor was leasing trailers to people whose homes had been destroyed, and Mother had gone off with Rosie and Mary Ellen Williger to look at some models, even though Mrs. Williger didn't want to raze their old house to install the trailer and Rosie didn't like the idea of living in one of the trailer parks. The rain was so thick you could scarcely see across the street. I dug my knees out from under me and stared with distaste at the music resting on the piano ledge.

I had taken out my violin and begun practicing my Bartok exercises when I heard noises on the staircase. I glanced up through the railing to find Sarah and Jolie sitting on the landing in their underpants.

"Eeeee!" they exclaimed, catching my eye. Jolie raced to cover her pink breasts with her hands, and they scooted like mice back up the stairs.

"Go jump in the lake!" I screamed after them.

I returned to the notes on the page and tried to block Jolie and Sarah from my mind. Even though I wasn't very interested in the music, I was taking care to play accurately in case Father was listening. The exercise had no real tune, but after a few minutes, its unexpectedness began to hold my attention. If you thought the next note would be up a third, it would be a second or even somewhere down to an odd flat. There were chords all of a sudden with strange harmonies too. I should have clipped my nails before beginning, I realized, flattening my fingers so that only the soft tips touched the bridge.

When Bobby Rogers banged on the screen, I stopped to let him in. "*Ichi bon!*" He tipped his filthy army cap at me and scampered up the stairs, trailing mud. I was sliding my hand into the higher positions and back. Miss Rideaux had marked all the directions in her delicate pencil, but she would be surprised by my skill. She never believed that I could read the notes and then put my fingers exactly there, no matter where they were on the treble clef.

I fished around for the new Brahms arrangement she had given me. The music was meant for piano and cello, but another composer had fixed the notes for the violin. The piece began as if already in the middle. I couldn't tell if Brahms had wanted it that way. It was a sonata, with a grownup sound, something yearning and sorrowful but insistent. Here and there chords gave it special strength. For some reason I thought Grandmother would have liked it. Maybe it was the melancholy running like a dark stream beneath the surface. As I placed two fingers down at once and drew my bow across the strings, I pictured her face, lined and wrinkled, her false teeth too perfect and the gums an odd shade of pink. Her permanented hair had stuck out in awkward flattened gray curls, because she had hated to comb it. Her scalp was too sensitive, she said, and she wrapped a hairnet around her head each night to protect the permanent until her next visit to Marilyn Sue's Mother.

The music had a soft tender passage, cut through with brisk chords, which I could see coming up on the next page; and then, as I entered the section, I heard in my ear the discordant piano accompaniment. One day, sitting together in the park near the band shelter, I had asked Grandmother how Grandfather had died. "So many people," she had said, looking far away, "so *viele Leute*," so that I had thought she wasn't answering, and still wasn't sure even after she had gone on. "*Von unserer Familie vielleicht dreissig.* Maybe thirty of our own family." Her words were a thorny tangle of German and English as she went on, and though I usually understood whatever she said, I could hardly follow. From Vienna, many of our people were taken away, "to the east." It was the year after she had left Vienna alone, ahead of her husband, the year after I was born. And they all had been killed, nearly all—the ones who hadn't gotten out. "You were already a baby," she said, as I scraped my shoe along the dirt beneath the bench, wondering if there were something that, being alive, I ought to have done. Grandmother sounded angry at her husband and those other relatives I had never met, as if they had been stupid, or done something wrong, to get themselves in such terrible trouble. "*Sie sagen*, they went like sheep to the slaughter," Grandmother said, using the English, "sheep to the slaughter," and a horrible smile, more like a terrible wince, showed her gold teeth. "Don't say your Mother I told you this. *Sagt nichts*, Eva, *Ja!*" she admonished, and her sallow lips parted into another odd smile, one that wavered between solicitousness and scorn. "I won't tell," I promised, looking off toward the creek in the distance with its odd sign underneath the bridge. What she had told me was more like dark dust clouds than a story in my mind. I wasn't glad to have heard it, though it buzzed like a worrisome insect in my brain.

"Eva!" Father was shouting angrily from somewhere in the house.

"What?" I said, but directed my attention to the music.

"Can't you keep tempo?"

"If you're not playing with me, you don't have a right to say anything," I snapped back.

Father didn't pay attention to anyone, even Mother, these days, but he still thought he could rule the house. I put down my violin and rested it on my knee. "Like sheep to the slaughter," I thought, hearing Grandmother's strange words, but picturing the horses running along Kansas Avenue. Was there anything I should be doing not to be a sheep in my house?

Father appeared beside me, munching an apple. "Don't you concentrate when you play?" he asked sarcastically. He bit out a large section and chewed noisily. "I shouldn't have to sit with you to get you to count."

"Don't worry," I answered, cocking my head.

"It's criminal to play Brahms the way you do," he went on, all worked up.

"It is not," I said, afraid to be answering him back twice in a row. Still, Grandmother's words were in my mind. "If you call wrong notes a crime, you're exaggerating," I pointed out.

Father leaned over the piano bench and struck a chord with his strong hands. He looked as though he might sit down and begin to play along with me. He played the chord again, almost pounding it into the piano; then he pointed to the music sheet and said, "Begin again here, and play to the end, this time in tempo."

He hadn't even heard what I had said.

We were all driving the Willigers to their condemned house on the other side of the Kaw. I hadn't wanted to come along. I saw enough of the Willigers in our house. "It'll be good for you to see where they live. Then you'll understand why they're staying with us." Mother had given me a meaningful look that didn't make the trip more tempting. But Father had finally ended the discussion. "This is a family outing. Everyone is going." It was the first time Mary Ellen Williger and Jolie were returning to their old home since they had escaped from the rising Kaw. I suspected Mrs. Williger would be forced to decide not to rebuild on their own property. She had made us frankfurters and beans for lunch but she hadn't been able to eat. Now she sat silently, looking small and hurt, between Father and Rosie in the front seat of our car. The two men were talking quietly. Rosie was saying he hadn't liked the trailers and thought he should hold out for a prefabricated home. It wouldn't take that much longer once the parts arrived, he told Father, as long as he went ahead and poured the concrete basement. You could tell Mary Ellen Williger was keeping herself from suggesting that they rebuild their old house.

Jolie had been silly all morning, and she and Sarah had dawdled so long over their lunch that Mother had to wrap up their half-eaten hot dogs. In the car, they peeled away the thin skins. Squealing with silly delight, they shook the naked pink frankfurters at each other.

"Pipe down," said Mother. This was a new American phrase she had learned that summer.

Jolie and Sarah quieted, but they were still dangling the ragged hot dogs before each other.

"*Ach*," said Mother. "Please eat your frankfurters."

"Jolie!" Mrs. Williger admonished, without turning back.

Mother leaned toward the front seat, holding the empty buns on her lap. "I never make this for my children," she said coolly; she must have thought herself too harsh, given Mary Ellen Williger's distress, for she added, as if to me, "Still, it was quite a treat, wasn't it, to have such special baked beans!"

"That's how they made them at the church picnic," I told her politely.

After a while Mother asked me to sit between the two girls. But this only made them sneak flops of their hot dogs across my face or behind my back.

"Efa, you're being very grown up," Mother tried to console me.

I pushed my glasses onto my nose and stared ahead at the passing buildings. I knew if I let go for an instant I would punch Jolie or Sarah as hard as I could.

We turned left onto Kansas Avenue and drove down the wide street toward the river. A few store fronts were still boarded up and caked high with trash-filled mud. In some shops people were nailing up new siding or installing a new glass window pane. A huge brown WATER SALE! sign had been papered over the front of a store. But the sale didn't look very promising. As we crossed the Kansas Avenue bridge, we could see the meat packing plant leaning tumbledown into the Kaw below. The river had subsided and was flowing tiredly in its deep bed, but both grayed banks were completely littered with broken furniture and planks.

"Too bad they're closing the plant," said Father.

"Euuu!" Sarah reached behind me to tickle Jolie. "Horse meat!"

I slapped her hand.

"You remember when we saw the runaway horses?" Mother tried to distract Sarah.

"They would have had to close it anyway, sooner or later," Rosie was saying to Father. "That plant was too small. Also, they specialized mostly in hogs, and the pork business is down." He had his arm relaxed out the open window and his hairs glistened copper in the warm sun.

"Still, over a thousand jobs," Father shook his head.

"That's not all that'll be out of work if they keep up that strike over at the Goodyear plant," Rosie mused.

"But the strike at Goodyear is partly because men were laid off."

The sun shining through the car window lay changing golden stripes across Father's face.

"Yeah, but they wouldn't have got laid off in the first place if some of the men hadn't gotten greedy and pushed their wages too high."

"I thought you were a union man," Father smiled quizzically.

"Not really. I figure, it's between every man and his boss. And if you're willing to work, you're bound to get paid."

Father thumped on a sun blossom on the steering wheel.

"Isn't your railroad work unionized?" he asked after a while.

"You're thinking of the union of porters and sleeping car workers. That's just for coloreds."

We drove through North Topeka, where used clothing stores, pawn shops, and cheap suppliers lined the Avenue. An empty marquee announced a theater that had once played sexy movies. Even before the flood, this part of town had been strange and rundown. Where the owners hadn't bothered to board up their stores, glass now littered the street and the brick and wood storefronts were turned askew. In some shops, you could see Negro men working to clear the debris. Several men leaned against a ragged wall, bandannas over their heads, to drink from glass bottles.

"I think it's mostly Jewish people that owns the stores along here," said Rosie.

"Yah?" Father glanced curiously out his sunny window.

"The pawn shop and the jewelry stores anyway. I heard tell they was supposed to be getting money from some big Jewish agency back east."

"I don't know anything about that."

"Well, you folks sure do take care of you own, that's all I can say," Rosie nodded with cautious respect.

"We also try to help other people," said Mother. She was holding her purse as she looked out the window.

"You know, for the longest time, we didn't even realize you folks was Jewish." Mrs. Williger gave her whinny laugh. "I mean, we knew you were from the other side. But you don't act any different, so I was real surprised when Mrs. Rogers told me."

"I'm sorry you only remember hearing it from Mrs. Rogers," Mother responded tensely. "I certainly thought we'd said something at dinner that first night. But Hitler said it: we're Jews."

"We were Jews before Hitler," Father said gruffly. "He certainly didn't make us something we weren't before."

"Well, the Lord helps those who help themselves," Mrs. Williger said softly.

"There may still be agencies back east organized to help refugees," said Father. "We were helped by one. They might also give money to people who were flooded, though I don't think they restrict themselves to Jews."

As Rosie pointed to a side street, Father swung the car onto a narrow road lined with small houses that looked as though they had been smashed by a haphazard wrecking crane.

Beyond the tight line of Mother's troubled cheek, an old brick school building, a quarter the size of mine, stood cramped but intact on a treeless lot. In the second-floor windows, children had taped pictures like those on the windows of my school. The rubble people had cleared from the sides of the building stood piled at the curb and the small scraped lot was muddy and empty of green. Two little girls with tiny black pigtails spiking outward all over their heads were jumping rope by the locked front door.

"That's the colored school," Rosie pointed with his sturdy hand.

"Is that where Mrs. Johnson's children go to school?" I touched Mother's arm.

"It could be," she nodded, but she was keeping her eyes on the window.

"Now that was a half-cocked idea, that integration they were trying to put across here earlier this summer," Rosie said. "Colored people and white people, they aren't alike. It'd be like putting wolves and chickens in the same pen." He must have hoped to smooth over the earlier moment of difference between him and Father about unions by drawing us into a common plight.

"Which is which?" Father gave a nasty laugh.

"Well, now the colored man, I've seen him on the job. So I'm not talking from prejudice. First, he won't put in a day's work. Then, when he does get paid, what does he think about? Fighting and drinking and you know what. Whereas the white man, he don't mind a fight, he's no coward, but he won't kill for fun."

"I'm afraid I don't agree," Mother said quickly, her voice trembling.

"Remember, colored folks were slaves less than a hundred years ago. You're new to this country, so there's history you may not yet be acquainted with. I've even heard tell they've got cannibal blood you can't get out, not that I—"

"*Quatsch!*" Mother responded, holding her purse tightly.

"Well, at least you got to give them time."

"I suspect they would tell you they've already waited too long," Father said sharply.

"Mrs. Johnson's sister-in-law is a teacher and Mayella reads as much as I do!" I leaned forward to add my facts to the argument, then, quivering inside, fell back on the seat.

"I don't know," Rosie shook his head genially. "Like I say, they're still more animal than human. Some white folks'll tell you that the colored man thinks like us. But it's not so. There ain't no way a white person can understand what a colored one is thinking or feeling."

"Most men can't imagine the thoughts of their wives and best friends," Father said bitterly.

"All people are alike, under the sun," Mother asserted her familiar opinion, but her voice shook and she sounded afraid.

"Anyway, I suspect this isn't the best day for a political discussion," said Father in a voice that made clear the little talk was now over.

As we drove along a mud road, the suddenly silent car was thick with tension—even Jolie and Sarah were sitting bolt upright in expectation of what might come next. It was hard to imagine that Mother and Mr. Williger had ever been friends.

"Oh, my!" Mrs. Williger cried out, touching her little cross. A gaping hole lay in a rubble-filled lot, as if someone had begun to dig a deep swimming pool in the midst of the mess. "That was a house over there. Mrs. Belford's from our church."

We stopped on a dead-end street of twisted one-story houses. Whole pieces had been chopped out and were scattered about among broken furniture and debris. A bird cage lay on its side, half-buried in the mud.

"No!" Jolie leaped up and hung over her mother.

"That's ours," Mrs. Williger nodded at a wooden house that leaned sideways toward the next lot. The windows were broken inside their frames, and the front door, pasted over with a yellow CONDEMNED strip, hung slantwise on its hinge.

"Now don't get upset," Rosie Williger instructed his wife.

"Oh Lord, where's the barn?" Mrs. Williger exclaimed as Jolie scrambled out of the car. "Honey, you didn't tell me that."

"You be careful," Mr. Williger called after his daughter. He took his wife's thin elbow and started walking toward their house.

"I don't want her touching anything, especially that stale water. She could get polio. Tell her, honey," Mrs. Williger begged her husband as he stooped to pick up a stray coffee pot.

I looked at the house which had once been a pale blue. On one side a red roof peeked out but it sloped downward and appeared to end up somewhere inside a room to the right of the front door. It didn't look like a home anybody would want to fix.

"*Shrecklich!*" Mother clicked her tongue. "We thought we lost everything, but look at this." She gave Father a frightened searching look.

"Some guests you invited into our house," he said, and turned as if to follow the Willigers.

"David!"

"Their abominable opinions don't make this any less awful." He said more gently as he waved an arm over the wrecked silt-covered yard. An old refrigerator leaned against a side window, left by the Willigers or deposited in the wake of the Kaw.

"Prejudice always arises out of people's own fears," Mother recited, half to me.

"Please, don't try to give explanations," Father warned angrily.

Mother's face was moving in ugly contractions. She seemed to need Father to put his arms around her or take her hand; yet I was afraid that, if Father stayed near her, he would begin to shout in an awful way.

"You don't think the children should know why we take in people who talk like this?" she suddenly demanded. She placed her hands on her hips and her sensible shoes gripped the mud.

"There are some things that don't yield to pleasing explanations, Leah," Father hissed.

Quickly, I took Mother's hand.

Rosie was unhooking the front door; it swung like a loose tooth as he eased himself in after Mrs. Williger. A moment later, Father followed them into the house.

"People are prejudiced because they're afraid. They use their prejudice to cover their fears," Mother repeated shakily.

"But they're not prejudiced deep down?" I asked.

Mother winced.

"So are we going to ask them to leave our house?"

Shaking her head, Mother fumbled in her pocket for a handkerchief and wiped her eyes. "Daddy is upset too," she said.

Jolie and Sarah had gone around to the long narrow backyard that ended in muddy debris clinging like rotten vines to a fence. Near the fence, a single reddish wall and a rough heap of boards indicated where a small barn had probably dropped noiselessly under water.

"You see?" she said ambiguously.

"You're not prejudiced when you're afraid," I noted, and loosened my hand.

"I really think we should let the Willigers alone while they see their home for the first time," decided Mother.

"Daddy's already gone in." I turned to cross the grimy front yard. It was hard to follow the walk, and only the most meager of spindly bushes poked green by the broken door. Still, I agreed with Father: nothing in their wrecked house could make right what Rosie had said.

Inside, I forgot about everything in the face of a sight I had never before seen. Tattered shades had been lowered, perhaps by

Rosie on one of his trips home, and torn curtains hung heavy with filth from their bent rods. An enormous once velvet couch of now indistinguishable color sat slimy and sponge-like at one end of the nearly evacuated living room whose floors pitched and fell and were so slippery and soft you had to be careful of each step.

Father was shaking his head in some dark internal conversation as he walked past me unseeingly and out the front door.

The next room opened out like an ordinary dining room with a large wooden table filling the floor, but half way across a lamp dangled precariously and the ceiling began to slope downwards, bulging and cracking, until at the edge of the table it pitched forward in a pool of wet plaster and broken boards. The far window had been squeezed like a used tin can; its barely parted mouth let in only a skim of light. Mrs. Williger was blowing her nose.

"Tell me what I did wrong!" she cried.

I picked up a shard of pottery and rubbed off the mud on my shorts, exposing tiny pink flowers.

"Honey, we'll get you a new one." Rosie Williger put his strong sunburned arm around his wife's frail shoulders.

Mrs. Williger sniffed over her handkerchief at me, "Just tell me where else could I have put the cabinet."

"It wasn't your fault. There wasn't nowhere safe," he told her.

"I never thought it was in a dangerous place. If I'd a known—" she said to me, blinking.

I tried to break past the poison inside me to smile encouragingly. "I'm sorry."

Mother had come into the room. Her eyes were red and her handkerchief was still in her hand. "*Ach!*" She put her hand over her mouth in horror.

"This was my mother's china cabinet."

"Mary Ellen had a real nice collection, with some pieces that were genuine antiques."

"We had the cabinet since we got married," Mrs. Williger cried out, showing the black hole in her mouth. "My mother gave it to us as a wedding present. I don't suppose there was anything else I ever cared about, really."

The cabinet only peeped out here and there from where it had gotten stuck under the roof, and its shattered glass lay mixed among the wreck.

Mother shook her head, and her red eyes matched Mrs. Williger's. "Before David's mother left Vienna, the Nazis came. They just marched in and scooped all her silver and china into a sheet and took it away." She tried to laugh.

I was embarrassed at Mother bringing in her own concerns, especially with people who would be unlikely to respect them. "What was this?" I offered Mrs. Williger my little flowered shard.

"Oh honey, that was a little cup—Spode." She wiped her eyes.

"Spode?"

"That's a very fine china," said Mother. "We had some too, in Vienna."

"You could see those flowers even when the cup was full of tea," Mrs. Williger explained. "I should have put the cups somewhere else."

"Can I have it?"

"Well, it's not good anymore."

"Isn't it dangerous to be in here?" Mother peered worriedly at the roof which had sliced off the room.

"No, not in daylight," said Rosie Williger, and lifted his arm from Mrs. Williger's shoulder to move a board. "Besides, I turned off the electricity."

I walked out of the dining room, back past the room with the sodden couch, into a little room that must have been Jolie's, for slime-covered dolls leaned against the wall. The dolls were so dark they looked like Negroes and reminded me of Mrs. Johnson, whose house must be like this. We had never gone to help her clean. A soggy mattress lay curled on rusted springs. The bedding had come to our house in one of Rosie's wet loads. I wandered through the kitchen, where the sink was filled with dishes packed in mud and the roof ducked down in one corner, leaving a treacherous cave between it and the messy floor. An open space marked where the back door had been. I went out.

Jolie and Sarah were poking at the sunny wood pile that had once housed Big Joe. They looked like dowsers with their long sticks. Sarah saw me and came running.

"Look." I held out my broken cup. "Spode. It's a special kind of china. Mrs. Williger's china cabinet got smashed by the roof."

"We found a dead chicken," Sarah squinted uncomfortably.

"I guess they won't be able to live here," I said, feeling a sickly sorrow for these people who might well hate us, if they weren't staying in our house.

*T*he dinner after our trip to North Topeka, Mrs. Williger brought in a surprise bakery cake, white with snowy glaciers of sugary frosting, and Mother was extra gay and friendly and everyone laughed and ate the cake. Yet Sarah had made me promise not to tell that out in back by the Williger's tumbledown barn, Jolie had said, "Jews smell bad."

"People grow up with strange ideas they don't even question," Father explained sadly, as he sat at my bed. Mother had sent him up to the attic because she knew I was upset.

"I thought you said some things don't have explanations!" I responded, recalling his harsh outcry at Mother.

Father sighed. "But let's talk a little. Maybe it would calm you to talk."

"Don't act like a doctor," I shot back. I didn't want that terrible glob of pain in my chest squeezed into tidy logical words.

"All right. But you might feel better."

I was beginning to cry, despite myself. Did he really want me to feel good about what I had seen and heard? Through my tears, I watched Father stand up to search for Kleenex tissues.

Returning to my bed, he handed me one. "Eva, we all have to get through the next weeks."

"Why?" I blew my mucus-filled nose into the tissue.

"Because we'll finish something we've begun, and your mother would never kick them out."

"What about you?"

Father rocked slowly on the bed. He took off his glasses and checked them for smudges and, wincing, set them back on his nose.

"But why does everyone have to pretend that no one has said anything wrong?" I cried out.

Several days later, with no end to the pretending in sight, I went off on my own in the late afternoon to pick up Father at the State Hospital. I was to meet him in Building H, to the left of the winding roadway, beyond the one low building that housed the canteen. A curtain of trees, followed by shady stubbled lawn, set the buildings with their long grilled windows back from Sixth, where I had gotten off the bus, and created isolated, high, red brick fortresses. I had been to the state hospital before with Father, when he went to see patients who had been transferred there, and I knew to read the thick black letters set out on a post on the grass before each heavily secured entrance. Even outside, the air smelled eerie: earlier it had been like walking past macaroni and cheese baking, but the wind had either changed or the few paces I'd gone had made the difference, and now it was more like laundry hampers filled with sour unwashed clothes.

The odd thing was that our pretending seemed as much about the Williger's wrecked home as about the prejudiced things that had been said during the trip there. Although I now took seriously the terrible luck that had struck the Willigers, neither they nor Mother remained saddened beyond the day of our visit to their house. It wasn't only that Rosie Williger was once again Mother's dream man, happily throwing himself into garden work, but everyone but me had decided to begin again without a word. No one mentioned either the Negro school or the little muddy street where the Willigers had once lived. No one asked them whether living in our house was going to change their hurtful notions of Jews. Perhaps the internationally famous minister Mrs. Rogers talked about was "fixing" everything for Mrs. Williger, who now spent hours across the street in front of the T.V. I couldn't guess how Mother had put aside all the cruel words she knew had been said. I was the only one for whom the Sunday trip lingered. I agreed I could no longer be selfish about having my own room, yet I couldn't rest easy in our crowded home. Perhaps my stubborn memory was my worst fault.

The key was to stay clear in one's mind and certain of what was right, I decided as I looked up fearfully into the barred windows. I was afraid of meeting the gleaming eyes of a patient staring back down at me.

I began to run across the clotted lawn, but a new fear came over me that someone would think I was a patient trying to escape and I slowed down to a gawky skip, feeling the uneven earth under my shoes. Water had worn away the ground in rivulets and exposed hard stony protrusions beneath the wet soil. A green hospital van turned into a driveway that led to the sunken back entrance of Building F. As I crossed the driveway, two uniformed attendants jumped out. From inside the truck, they pulled a thin ageless man in vast gray overalls with sharp features and a shaven head. Pointing, the man tried to lunge in my direction, but the attendants hurried him in the back door.

Why had I begged to be allowed to pick up Father alone, while Sarah and Jolie helped Mother and Rosie trim back the dead branches of a lilac bush? I wondered, as my stomach turned queasy. I had watched them a while from the bathroom window, heard Mother's laughter and Jolie's "Eh-eh-eh-heh-eh" woodpecker cry, which Sarah tried to imitate. I wished I were back at the edge of the grounds where I had gotten off the bus, but now there was nowhere left to go but further in. Building G was on my right. For a moment, I wasn't sure whether Building H was behind it or over more to the side. High boxwood obscured the grilled first floor windows. I didn't even see the canteen.

"Eva!" someone was calling. The voice swept over me like a chilly wind and I was afraid to turn around.

"Eva! Is that you?"

I halted and looked fearfully about. Mordecai was coming down a narrow walk in his seersucker suit, his pipe protruding from his dark beard. I wanted to rush toward him and hold on for dear life. . . But what about Father? Would he be angry if I talked to Mordecai? What did I have to do to be loyal to him? I took a deep jagged breath and kept my attention on my feet until I was nearly there. "Hi." I glanced up at Mordecai's black eyes and the soft mouth that held the sweet-smelling pipe.

"What are you doing here all alone?"

"Father's at a special meeting in Building H," I blushed.

"I was there myself. But they weren't coming to any decisions, so I volunteered to make a tour of those Menninger patients who've been transferred here. Now do you know your way around?" Mordecai rested his warm long fingers on my shoulder.

"I think so."

"Come, I'll go with you."

We began walking briskly together, Mordecai and I, as if we ourselves were old friends.

"Mordecai," I asked, wanting to unburden my untroubled mind, but afraid to talk directly about the Willigers, "Did Noah take both Jews and Christians into the ark?"

"Now why do you ask that?" He took his pipe from his mouth and a soft grin appeared in his beard.

I shrugged sheepishly.

"Well, there weren't any Christians at the time, you know," he said. "There wouldn't be for several thousand years."

"But what about Negroes? Did he take any of them?"

"That's a good question," Mordecai laughed. "The story of Noah is from a time when the world of the rabbis was very small."

"But were there Negroes?"

"Yah, there must have been."

"And were they saved?"

"It's an apocryphal story. I don't suppose the flood covered the whole world, even though the Bible said it did. The way the story goes, Noah had three sons. They and their wives were taken into the ark, and when the waters receded, the sons each went in a different direction and their children became all the nations."

"But the people who lived together didn't think in different ways."

"No, not in the ark, I suppose. Not more than in any family." He looked at me thoughtfully and sucked his pipe.

"But still, the people who had suffered in the flood went out into the world—" I was proceeding slowly, trying to keep my thought narrow and straight. "I mean, after a while, they forgot that they had suffered and became prejudiced against each other."

"You might say, they forgot they were once relatives. I doubt suffering decreases prejudice. Who told you that?" Mordecai shook his head.

"Mother," I said, feeling caught. "Because of the war, that's why she knows everyone's really alike, deep down."

"Well, unfortunately not everyone who escaped from Europe drew the same lesson," Mordecai laughed, as he came to a stop under a tree. "There are lots of Jews who are as bigoted as anyone else. And then, about being the same, 'deep down,' of course your mother is partly right, but I'd also say everyone is different—which is what makes us interesting to each other."

I kept still but placed my hands in my pockets, a little afraid.

"It's marvelous to notice differences among people," he continued. "It's why our world is so awesome. I'm different from you. Your father is different from me. What makes the thought dangerous is when it's followed by a second thought: I'm better than you, or, my way's better." He nodded. "People often aren't very careful when they notice the differences between themselves and another, and they rush to judge their own way best, which causes trouble."

"Maybe that's because the difference makes them afraid. Mother said fear makes people prejudiced," I reported.

"Possibly, though I don't think you can boil prejudice down to a single psychological cause. You have to look at economics— what kinds of people have what kinds of jobs."

"Mordecai, do you feel proud of being Jewish?" I tentatively asked.

"Well, of course," Mordecai laughed. "I wouldn't want to be anything else!"

"I don't," I admitted, embarrassed.

I could feel the dry warmth of his slim hand as it slipped through mine and we began again to walk.

"I bet your mother does," he said, after a time.

"But Mother says Jews should act like everyone else. She said those Jews who dressed in a special way irritated Hitler!"

"Then your mother herself has a kind of prejudice. That surprises me," Mordecai said, and puffed on pipe. "It's what many assimilated Ashkenazi Jews believed. They thought, if only

Jews acted like good Germans or good Austrians, we wouldn't provoke the anger of the gentile population. But Hitler rose to power in Germany, and Nazism was most virulent in Austria. So does giving up our difference really help?"

He wasn't really asking me. I ran along quietly beside him, straining to keep up.

"In my father's *stetl*, when Jews tried to explain Hitler's growing power, they said just the opposite from your mother. They blamed those Jews who had tried to assimilate. 'If we had kept to ourselves and held to our ancient ways,' they said, 'we would now be safe.' But they were wrong too." He gripped my hand harder. "You can't explain what happened in Europe by our behavior. We can't be made responsible for what *they* did to us."

I shivered; the trees blew a warm wind that gave little relief.

"But does God want there to be suffering?" I suddenly wanted to know.

The pipe was back in the corner of his mouth as Mordecai gave a melancholy laugh. "You ask questions that are hard to answer so simply. I suppose one of the differences among people is in the way we think of God."

"But it doesn't seem fair that He would allow poor people, or Negroes—or Jews," I added cautiously, "to suffer especially much."

"Fair," Mordecai repeated, nodding his dark head.

"Wouldn't a God want the world to be nice for everyone?"

"I'll tell you something," Mordecai said, and his fine hand suddenly held mine neither too loose nor too tight. "Some people, like my Father—who, incidentally was one of those Hasidic Jews your mother spoke of so disrespectfully—people like my father, even as they went off to the gas chambers prayed, 'My God, your world is perfect!' And they may have been right. While others, like your father, look at what was done to the Jews, or the way Negroes live in this country, and say, 'Even if there is a God, I couldn't pray to the One who would allow such evil.' And they may be right. The point is, many wise men have tried to understand human corruption and suffering and, although there are answers that satisfy some, the question still seems unanswerable, and we still have to live with the pain of what we see everyday."

"Lillian said that the evil of the world was responsible for the flood," I remembered.

Mordecai nodded. "You know she's here now? She and a few other patients are why we had our meeting."

"Is she okay?" I asked.

"I don't think so. She doesn't get much help here. But people at Menninger's generally felt we couldn't do anything for her there anymore either."

"Even Hans?"

"Hans just reported objectively what went on in his talks with her. He let the others decide."

"I liked Lillian a lot." I looked up at Mordecai. "I used to stop to talk to her."

"You could visit her here sometimes, if you wanted."

I slowed down beside him; the thought of seeing Lillian in the midst of a whole ward of women as crazy as she made me dizzy.

"Actually, you could come along with me. I could take you there now." Mordecai stopped and looked down at me.

"What about Daddy?"

"The meeting won't be over for a while."

We walked quickly past the canteen and Building H, where Father would still be sitting with Hans and the other doctors, then down a hillock lined with a clump of pines. Somewhere, ahead of us, the river was finally flowing quietly inside its bed. Mordecai's words were drifting into a fog of confusion as the prospect of seeing Lillian filled my mind. I had never been inside one of the state hospital buildings. My legs were mushy as we climbed the wide entrance steps. From the front hallway came the odor of disinfectant, threatening and burning. Behind a battered desk, an enormous blotchy-faced woman sat reading her newspaper. She glanced up to give Mordecai a brief nod. Then an attendant in a crisp white uniform unlocked an elevator with one of the large heavy silver keys that dangled from his pocket. As the elevator slowly ground upward, I stood close to Mordecai. The smoke from his pipe floated around me, comforting yet disturbing.

"You're okay, aren't you?" he smiled.

"I think so."

"I wonder if your father will be angry at me for bringing you here."

I shook my head vigorously, though I wasn't at all sure what Father would say.

We stood at the edge of a large hall that looked like a railway station with light filtering in from high windows. Women of all shapes rocked and mumbled to themselves on the long benches. The air smelled of dust and old sweat, as if it were filled with dozens of Anna Mandelbaums or refugees from the church basement. The attendant had locked himself back in the elevator and I could see the little caged window descending. I made my breathing shallow and reached for Mordecai's comforting hand.

A bony woman was sidling up to me. "What's your name? Oh, I'm so sorry!" she said, jerking her head as if someone invisible were slapping her.

"Eva," I replied.

"Sorry, sorry." The woman hid her face in the collar of her slack hospital dress.

"There's Lillian," Mordecai pointed, pulling me forward.

As we wended our way among the benches, I caught sight of a woman bent over a large bag. She sat at the side of the room, by one of the high windows, squeezed into her ragged cotton uniform. In the dusty light, her hair shone red at the fringes. But during the two last months since I'd seen her, coarse gray hair had filled in most of her head. Dirty and rumpled, Lillian looked as though she had put on an unironed dress and then slept in her clothes.

"Hi, Lillian. Here I am, Mort Stone—you remember, I said I would come. And this is Eva Hoffman. You know Eva from Menninger's."

Lillian glanced up suspiciously. Her green eyes darted back and forth between us, as they had when she was still at Menninger's, but her whole face was contorted by a twitch that pulled at her mouth. "I know you," she whispered to Mordecai. It's that Mandelbaum I don't want to see."

Mordecai nodded. "Still, I know he misses you and will come to visit."

"Psss!" Lillian hissed at him angrily, jerking her head to scare us away. She wouldn't look at me.

I was holding Mordecai's hand and sweat was forming a little trickle in my closed palm.

"Now you be nice. These here are visitors," said a Negro attendant who had come up behind us. The man leaned over gently to straighten the wrinkled collar of Lillian's dress.

"Why does that man touch me?" Lillian drew herself up haughtily, as if she were still a wealthy lady. But her face was twitching terribly.

"She's fine the way she is," Mordecai nodded at the man.

"It took four of us to restrain her. She had one of her bouts last night," said the attendant, who did have exhausted circles under his dark eyes. "She would have had all the toilets stopped with everyone's clothes. But we had her in cold packs until a few hours ago."

"Oh, what a shame!" Mordecai turned to Lillian. "I'm really sorry."

"This is all that's left," Lillian whispered hoarsely, snatching Mordecai's free hand.

"What are you talking about?"

She whispered something to herself, scarcely moving her lips, and her eyes were sharp green stones snapping out at the room.

"Come, talk to us. Let us know what you're thinking."

"Who betrayed us? Who thought himself mighty enough to decide?" Lillian hissed, as she surveyed the waste of women. Sun from the high window filtered the dust into a rainbow before us. "You think I'm stupid enough to believe that we were the ones saved?"

"Are you talking about the flood? Or your transfer to the state hospital?" said Mordecai. "The transfer, I know, you spoke about with Hans. As for the waters, you can probably see from your window: the river has gone down, leaving a lot of mud everywhere."

"Some people's houses were destroyed," I added, to provide her with information she might have missed.

"But you know your transfer had nothing to do with the flood," said Mordecai.

"Ha!" screeched Lillian, as if catching us in a lie.

"I know it's hard to believe when two terrible things come at once."

Lillian looked confused. Suddenly she turned to me and, trying to get hold of her twitching face, crowed, "You go to school, dear?"

"Yes. I'll be in fifth grade in September."

She said something to herself and flung her dirty fingers bird-like in the air. Then in the same sweet honey voice, she asked, "How old are you, dear?"

"I'm going to be ten," I answered nervously, "two weeks before school starts."

"Happy birthday," Lillian smiled, and her face opened into the old puffiness as her green eyes came alive with warm attention.

"Thanks."

"Is it hard to be ten dear?"

"Well, I'm not really ten yet." I glanced quickly at Mordecai.

"Too much to understand," she sighed and looked deeply into my eyes.

"Are any of your children ten?" I asked, remembering that she had three.

Her eyes continued to peer into mine. "No, older," she said slowly, and a terrible sorrow crossed her face.

"I'm so glad you're trying to keep your mind clear," Mordecai said to her.

Lillian turned to him gruffly. "What?" she screamed. "You can't trick me. I'm supposed to believe this is all that's left?" Her eyes shot about the room, her face pulling inward. "These aren't my people. I can't talk to them. Who put me here?" Her arms flung out as the skinny woman slithered past, eyeing us nervously.

"Get away from me!" Lillian screamed.

"I'm sorry, I'm sorry."

"Why are you mean to that lady?" I asked.

"Next time it'll be an explosion!" Lillian called after her. "And you won't even be one of the ones saved. What hell!" She crossed herself and looked at me.

"Well, I'm sorry I said anything about your mind," laughed Mordecai. "We can't stay long. I just wanted to check how you're doing and give Eva a chance to see you again."

"Happy birthday, Eva." Lillian stopped short and her voice was suddenly normal, neither too sweet nor screaming. Digging deep down into her worn shopping bag, she brought forth a lavender handkerchief decorated with a rainbow of crocheted lace dancing around the edges. "Happy birthday, Eva!" she repeated, laying the handkerchief on my hand and folding my fingers tightly over it.

I looked unsurely at Mordecai.

"Go ahead," he nodded, smiling. "It's an early birthday present from Lillian. Very pretty."

"Thanks, Lillian," I said.

I opened my fingers and studied the precious lavender handkerchief with the rainbow spider web around its rim. "Did you make it?"

"Before the flood," Lillian whispered hoarsely. She dug into her bag again and pulled out a spool of pink with a crochet hook inserted in the threads. "Got to get another hanky." She looked at me searchingly.

"I'll get you one. What color?"

Lillian studied me a moment. "You choose," she said.

"You're a healer," Mordecai smiled at me. "You bring her out, find her good and generous side."

"Moments of hope," Lillian mumbled below her breath.

"Thanks Lillian." My voice was shaky as I folded the handkerchief carefully to tuck in my dress pocket. "It's really pretty."

"How old did you say you're going to be, dear?" She scratched her ear.

"I'll be ten."

"Oh, my," said Lillian, and she seemed to want to break into her crazy contorted cackle, but she held her face straight and a moment later it relaxed as her eyes glistened at me.

"*C* ome, let's talk about your birthday." Mother pulled off her apron and led me toward the living room.

She sat down on the couch, and I rested on the edge of the coffee table before her.

"Shall we make you a little party?" she asked, taking my hand in hers.

"Who could we invite?"

"We have quite a big family here!" Her eyes sparkled behind her glasses.

I winced and touched Lillian's handkerchief deep inside the pocket of my shorts.

"You could also invite someone from school, if you like."

"Who?

"Efa, it's your decision. It's *your* birthday!"

"Everyone is on vacation in August," I lied, for I had seen Marilyn Sue the other day when I was riding my bike. "Anyway, all I want is my room back," I added, feeling that I was somehow contradicting Mordecai's puzzling message. What exactly had he said?

Mother leaned against the couch and laughed heartily. The summer heat had curled the stray ends of hair around her forehead and the nape of her neck, and her polka dot sundress made her look comfortable and contented.

"It's not as if it's even a present," I pointed out coyly, "because it's already mine. It was taken away."

Sitting there with Mother, I could picture the crinkly tissues of a shoe box: inside lay a pristine pair of patent leather shoes like Marilyn Sue had worn to church. The box sat on a pink table cloth covering a table out in the backyard. Next to it was a large chocolate cake with ten pink candles. Why was it so difficult to make the world nice?

"I'm certainly not starting school with them still here."

"I'm afraid school is compulsory in this country, young lady," she smiled and shook her head.

I pulled out the handkerchief and studied the rainbow threads at the edge of the lavender. Mother had wrinkled her nose at the colors, and Mrs. Williger, to whom I had shown the handkerchief, was even afraid to touch it because it had come from a crazy lady. But I loved it! It was perfect—my only present so far.

Actually, I dreaded my birthday. It was the same every year: birthdays made you want a day in which everything went just right, from the moment you woke up until you went to sleep at night. Breakfast should be exactly what you wanted: hot cross buns with sugary frosting. The weather should be fine, neither hot nor cold, but a gorgeous yellow sun in a sky so blue you could smell its sweetness. On your birthday, you should have friends who were exactly as you wanted them. And they should ring your front doorbell dressed in lovely party clothes, carrying beautifully wrapped presents. The presents should be exactly right—even if you hadn't thought of them beforehand. "Oh, how pretty! This is just perfect!" I would wear my special blue and white pinafore that matched my eyeglass frames. The pink tablecloth was in my mind again, with the frosted chocolate cake resting like a crown in the exact middle. People would wear pointed paper party hats and blow out the candles. And wouldn't it be wonderful if Lillian came to my birthday, all cleaned up and happy! Her hair would have to be dyed red again, of course. But I would tuck her handkerchief in my pinafore, and I would give her new ones to crochet around the borders. "Lillian, you're going to be just fine," I would say, and pat her hand. And Mrs. Johnson and her children—Mayella, Lebert, Edmund, and John Henry—would all come. They would be dressed in starchy new church clothes, and Mrs. Johnson's mouth would relax with pleasure. Then I would give Mayella some new books to read.

"What are you thinking?" laughed Mother.

I looked up at her broad-boned face, wrinkled with laughter, and suddenly tears were running down my cheeks.

"We'd better buy Lillian some handkerchiefs," I cried out.

"We will, *süsse*."

"But we never cleaned Mrs. Johnson's house!"

"Come here," said Mother, drawing me toward her.

"No." I hung back.

"I wish you would talk to your father."

"Talking doesn't help everyone," I said in despair. "Anyway, Daddy doesn't really listen anymore."

I got off the coffee table, bewildered and still sniffling. Wiping my eyes behind my glasses, I went into the kitchen, through the back porch, and out the back door. Father sat alone on a deck chair; he gave me a nod and returned to his book. I wouldn't even try to bother him. In the side yard, Sarah and Jolie were playing in the orange plastic swimming pool Mr. Williger had brought home as a special present. I didn't much feel like being with Sarah and Jolie, but I needed company. The two were jumping in and out of the little pool and splashing each other. Sarah had on a faded green bathing suit I had once worn. But Jolie was wearing nothing but her cotton underpants, and her nipples stuck out soft and pink. I walked slowly toward the pool and halted a distance away.

"You're getting a sunburn," I said, pointing to the bright pink on Jolie's freckled shoulders.

Jolie was undoing her braids in long crimson streamers. She looked down at her chest. "I don't care."

"It's going to hurt tomorrow."

"So what."

"Why don't you come in?" Sarah invited me. She sat in a corner, slapping her legs in the water. Little bits of yellow grass had been dragged into the pool. Despite all the rain, the grass was baking and drying out in the August sun.

I dabbled my fingers in the tepid water. I hadn't told Mother what I wanted for my birthday, and it would be my fault if the day turned out badly. But even if I got shiny patent leather shoes, where would I wear them?

Suddenly from the front yard Bobby Rogers came racing over and jumped into the pool. "*Ichi bon! Ichi bon!*" he yelled out. "*Ichi bon!*"

"What's with you, Trigger?" Jolie splashed at him.

"See anything new? See anything new?" he sang, kicking up his heels in the water. He still had on his tennis shoes, but he didn't seem to care. "You guys are blind! Wow! You're really blind."

"Bobby! Stop it!" cried Sarah. "Look at all that grass you brought in!"

"You got on a new army hat," I said. It was the same style as the last, a boat that opened up for his head, but this one was new and crisp and tan.

"My dad came home last night," Bobby said, and rubbed his suddenly red nose.

"How long is he staying?" asked Sarah.

"Don't know. His legs are in casts."

"Is he okay?" I asked, glancing at the Rogers' house. It looked utterly closed down and quiet across the street.

"I guess. I don't know if he can walk."

"Too bad he missed the flood," Jolie laughed. She didn't even notice that Bobby was working hard to keep from crying. She was laying a plank at the edge of the pool, and then she rocked on it like a seesaw until she fell in. Water splashed where I was standing and got my shoes and halter wet. Suddenly Bobby dashed out of the pool and jumped on the makeshift diving board, and again water sprayed all over.

"You're taking all the water out of the pool," I said, backing off still further.

"We fill it up whenever it gets empty," Sarah said calmly.

I looked down at my sprinkled clothes. Even with the grass in the water, I felt like cooling off. Sitting down on the lawn, I peeled off my shoes.

"Here, sit here." Sarah moved over to make room for me.

"I'll fill the pool up first." I went to the side of the house to turn on the hose. Holding the nozzle under the water of the plastic pool, I watched the clean new water ripple out and add to the old.

"Koreans eat monkey meat," Bobby Rogers informed us, as he concentrated on unlacing his soaked tennis shoes under the water.

"No, they don't," said Sarah.

"You don't know! My dad just told me."

"Spray me!" commanded Jolie, looking at me with her watery blue eyes.

I turned the hose on Jolie, moving the water up and down her legs, her white belly, her pudgy breasts, and her shoulders.

Then I dropped the hose into the pool and stepped in. I sat down next to Sarah and began hosing myself with the nozzle. The water was bringing goosebumps to my skin, but it felt refreshing. Bobby Rogers got out to put his streaming wet shoes on the grass. Jolie was relaxing on her back.

"This is like the Gage Park swimming pool," Sarah said contentedly.

There was a long pause, but it suddenly didn't seem peaceful; then Jolie laughed. "No it ain't." She was looking straight at me. "Because here we got to swim with Jew-Niggers. And they don't allow none there." Still staring at me, she scooped water toward Sarah.

For a moment I thought my body would explode. "Why?" I heard myself call out, as the ghost of Mordecai seemed to lurch off into the distance.

Sarah said, "That's not nice, Jolie," and tossed back water.

"Nice?" I cried.

Jolie's freckled body seemed to spread out and fill the whole pool. "Nice?" The water had suddenly turned muddy; it lay around me as dirty as the sewage pools at the waterworks. Why would someone talk like that? "Why?" I didn't know what I was going to do, but my mouth tasted filthy, and I felt like throwing up. "Why, why?" I shouted, rising out of the slimy water and stepping out of the plastic pool. "Why? Why?" I was shouting as I lifted the heavy plastic rim of the pool to my shoulder, rolling Jolie and Sarah downward and splashing torrents of water over them and the garden. "Why, why, why?" They were scrambling to their feet as I dropped the now empty pool and walked around the corner to the front of the house.

"Jolie didn't mean it!" I could hear Sarah yell after me. "Jolie, tell her you didn't." But I couldn't live through it again and again. "Why?" I was crying softly. "Why?"

Father had finished his reading and was sitting at the piano, looking through scores. "We have chamber music this evening," he called as I ran up the stairs. "Maybe you would like to practice a little to prepare."

"Why?" I sobbed out, though I knew he didn't hear.

In the bathroom, I leaned over the toilet as my lunch came up, and up. When my stomach felt dry and empty, I doused my pounding head with water. Then I filled a cup with cold water and rinsed out my mouth. Mordecai was wrong! Why did it happen over and over? Everywhere, on towel racks, above the sink, even on the lid of the toilet back, were cluttered signs of the Willigers. Why? There was no explanation, as Father had angrily said. The dirty feeling hadn't gone away. I pulled my toothbrush from the ceramic rack and began to scrub my teeth. "Why? Why?" And then, as I had a crazy idea, I felt relief. In my parent's closet, I found Mother's empty shopping bags. I took one up to my attic room. Even though it was late afternoon, the air was hot and dense and it was hard to breathe. From the hanger, I took my blue and white pinafore and a skirt and blouse for the first day of school. My summer pajamas were faded and torn, but I didn't have any others. At that moment, I realized I had forgotten about the lavender handkerchief when I'd gone in swimming. I pulled it out of my pocket. It was wet but okay. I straightened out the wrinkled colored border, pulled on a pair of dry shorts, and stuffed the handkerchief into my pocket. There were socks and *The Secret Garden*, that maybe someone who could imitate dialect would read to me at night, and a hairbrush— all went into the shopping bag. I wasn't sure where I was going, but I was getting out.

Climbing down the attic stairs, I was a little sorry to miss the chamber music evening. Micha and Hans would come and maybe Anna Mandelbaum, though I wouldn't miss her, and Mother would serve her special *pflaumenkuchen* with the freshly sliced plums. But I was sick of Father calling on me for music and ignoring me the rest of the time. At least Mordecai would be absent, because I didn't even want to talk to him. At the foot of the stairs I wondered if I should leave a note. But I didn't feel like telling them where I was going, and besides I didn't yet know where I'd be.

I tiptoed down toward the first floor, around the landing. At the foot of the steps, a sob came to my throat as I glanced into the kitchen where Mother stood rolling out dough. I could see a cold salad on the table, waiting to be eaten at dinner. But it would all start over again. I knew that by now. And no one else would get upset as I did. There wasn't any room left in the house for me. Father sat at the piano, singing that Mahler *lieder*.

Nun will die Sonn' so hell aufgeh'n
Als sei kein Unglück, die Nacht gescheh'n!

Now the sun will rise as brightly
as if no bad luck had occurred in the night.

He didn't see me as I quickly passed him on my way to the front door.

Das Unglück geschah nur mir allein!
Die Sonne sie scheinet allgemein!

The bad luck fell on me alone.
The sun shines everywhere!

Outside, I could hear Bobby Rogers explaining something to Jolie in the side yard and then he yelled, "*Ichi bon!*" If only Sarah and I were still close, I would tell her I was leaving, maybe take her along.

$\mathcal{I}$ had crossed Sixth, walked by the corner beauty parlor and then, further down the street, passed Marilyn Sue's house. By the park, I turned off towards school, wondering for a moment if Miss Woody might be there, and what she would have to say about how the summer had gone. Did she want Negro children to come to our school? A few boys were playing on the baseball diamond, but the school doors were locked and there was no sign of anyone. I didn't even know where Miss Woody lived. Turning the far corner, I passed the teeter-totters, jungle gyms and other equipment I'd played on when I was in the earlier grades. I'd been such a child—so mistaken about so many things—in those days. The houses were on both sides of the street once again. I didn't know exactly how the neighborhood went, beyond the school where I now was. But I felt emptied of all problems and strangely calm. I felt I could walk forever without growing tired, that walking itself was a place to be. Every so often I shifted my shopping bag, but even that wasn't a heavy load. Except for my book, I was traveling light. Mother had warned me not to talk to strangers and never to accept rides in cars of people I didn't know. Now that I'd heard Mordecai criticize Father, I wasn't even going to talk to a policeman.

But what was I going to do? I didn't really have a place to go.

I was on a street with large old houses and big wide lawns. Some children had a croquet game set up in a grassy side yard, and the crack of their mallets against the ball was lonesome in the cooling evening air.

I picked up my shopping bag to carry like a baby and pictured Father alone at his music. Would he be missing me now? Mother was probably already worried: she would have noticed I was gone. She would be asking Sarah to help look around, and maybe after a while they would dare to disturb Father at his piano. I hoped they would all feel sorry for the way things had gone; perhaps they would even make resolutions about how they might be different if I would come home.

It would be best if I could wait for everyone to change, I thought, as little houses, more like cabins, stood in clumps amidst unmowed grass as high as wheat. There was still a sidewalk, but now its cracks were filled with wild grass and clover. Some of the houses looked deserted, and all of them had the soggy look of having stood under water. Climbing up a slight incline, I crossed the railroad tracks as dusk was coming on. I was beginning to get tired. The opening gave out onto a vast sky that high in the west shone pink, laced over by thin clouds. And then, suddenly, through a copse of tall trees whose trunks were still crusted with mud, I glimpsed the widened gray river bank and beyond it the flowing Kaw river.

A pickup truck like Rosie Williger's, but older and more rickety, was parked at the edge of the bank. Its open back was piled with old tires, a baby carriage, wooden planks and pieces of steel. It looked as though someone were gathering all the stray objects the flood had left in its wake. Down by the water, I saw a thin old Negro man with dazzling white hair bend over as he yanked at something. I set down my shopping bag near the truck, where the bank grew soft; it had grown heavy on my arm. Then I wound my way down the mud to join the old man.

"What are you doing?" I asked.

Across the river, on our left, the sun was still visible, a gleaming tomato cut off at the bottom.

The man seemed to pull the thing free, and then he looked up.

"This is an old spring, but I don't know if I can get anything for it or not."

"Are you going to sell it?"

"If I can. Where you come from, Miss?" he asked, his eyes narrowing.

"My house. Are you going to sell everything in the truck?"

"What I can. The tires I keep."

I leaned into the water to help pull at the rusty spring.

"Be careful you don't hurt yourself," he said.

"What will you do with the tires?" I asked, standing back.

"Some I'll use for patching other tires, some for resoling shoes." He looked at me carefully, then up at the truck where my shopping bag stood waiting. "You on your way somewhere?" he asked suspiciously.

The sun had slid into the greenish gray fog on the other side of the river, where Mrs. Johnson and her family lived and the Williger's house stood empty.

"Where do you live?" I asked the man.

"In my truck."

"Do you know Mrs. Johnson?"

"Lot of Johnsons around here, Miss."

I felt in my pocket for the crinkly rainbow rim of the lavender hanky Lillian had given me.

"What you doing way out here, anyway?" He had pulled loose the spring and was dragging it along.

"I didn't like my house anymore."

"Ain't no home perfect, Miss." He scratched the tiny white curls on his dark head. "You know your address?"

"I could help you first," I said, though I was awfully tired.

Curbstone Press, Inc.

is a non-profit publishing house dedicated to literature that reflects a commitment to social change. Curbstone presents writers who give voice to the unheard in a language that goes beyond denunciation to celebrate, honor and teach. Curbstone builds bridges between its writers and the public – from inner-city to rural areas, colleges to community centers, children to adults. Curbstone seeks out the highest aesthetic expression of the dedication to human rights and intercultural understanding: poetry, testimonials, novels, stories, photography.

This mission requires more than just producing books. It requires ensuring that as many people as possible know about these books and read them. To achieve this, a large portion of Curbstone's schedule is dedicated to arranging tours and programs for its authors, working with public school and university teachers to enrich curricula, reaching out to underserved audiences by donating books and conducting readings and community programs, and promoting discussion in the media. It is only through these combined efforts that literature can truly make a difference.

Curbstone Press, like all non-profit presses, depends on the support of individuals, foundations, and government agencies to bring you, the reader, works of literary merit and social significance which might not find a place in profit-driven publishing channels. Our sincere thanks to the many individuals who support this endeavor and to the following organizations, foundations and government agencies: ADCO Foundation, Witter Bynner Foundation for Poetry, Connecticut Commission on the Arts, Connecticut Arts Endowment Fund, Ford Foundation, Greater Hartford Arts Council, Junior League of Hartford, Lawson Valentine Foundation, LEF Foundation, Lila Wallace-Reader's Digest Fund, The Andrew W. Mellon Foundation, National Endowment for the Arts, Puffin Foundation, and United Way-Windham Region.

If you'd like to support Curbstone's efforts to present the diverse voices and views that make our culture richer, tax-deductible donations can be made to Curbstone Press, 321 Jackson St., Willimantic, CT 06226. Telephone: (860) 423-5110.